THE GINSENG GANG

Bill Tucker

The Ginseng Gang
by
Bill Tucker

© 2014

ISBN: 978-1-936553-60-0

Cover painted by the author.

Warwick House Publishers
720 Court Street
Lynchburg, Virginia 24504

ACKNOWLEDGMENTS

I am deeply indebted to the following people who shared their knowledge and experience.

In no particular order, I want to thank Amherst County Sheriff, L. J. Ayers, Major Betty Wise and Cassandra Myers for taking the time to answer my many questions.

Thank you to Lynn Coffey for reading my manuscript and offering some very helpful suggestions. Lynn is a best selling author and was editor of the monthly newspaper *Backroads* for 25 years. Her books have been praised by Jan Karon, Earl Hamner and others.

Thanks also to Donald Johns, president of Conner Produce in Lynchburg. He shared his vast knowledge of the produce business and how it is shipped and distributed around the country.

There are several colorful people who have shared their unique experiences when moonshine was in its heyday. First, John Moore Wright worked for the Virginia Department of Alcoholic Beverage Control for 30 years. Before retirement, he served as director of the Enforcement Division for 17 years. As director, he supervised 145 law enforcement personnel as well as a support staff of 30. He has an arsenal of stories about chases, raids and unusual characters and experiences.

Next is my friend Morris Stephenson, who is still working as a reporter with The Franklin County *News-Post*. In earlier careers he served as editor/publisher of *The Franklin County Times* and then 17 years with NASCAR before returning to *The News-Post*. In the early days Morris had the only camera locally that could produce pictures for the newspaper. Therefore, revenue agents would call him when they wanted to record a still bust. Over time, Morris came to know the men and women on both sides of the law. He knew the makers, transporters, state and local police, ATF agents and the state revenue agents. He has also written a book, *A Night of Makin' Likker*.

Morris introduced me to a couple of people and told me about others. One of the most interesting revenue agents and storytellers was Jack Allen Powell. Unfortunately, Jack died in 2013, but he had written several books about busting stills, working undercover, wild chases and getting shot at. Jack occasionally had problems for sometimes pushing the envelope too far, or using methods that were not always the approved method of operation, but he truly loved busting stills.

Special thanks to Joyce Maddox and Amy Moore of Warwick House Publishers for their guidance and expertise in helping me get this book published.

Finally, I especially want to thank Darrell Laurant for critiquing my book. Darrell is a well-known author/writer/journalist. His columns and articles in *The News and Advance* in Lynchburg, Virginia, have been treats for many years. His suggestions and recommendations were invaluable.

CHAPTER 1

On an early cold fall morning, two hikers walking down Spruce Creek Road found the man lying in a shallow ditch. He was curled up in the leaves in a fetal position looking like road kill. They were sure he was dead. A Bluetick hound was lying behind him with his head resting over his right shoulder. The dog gave a deep throaty growl when they tried to approach. Dried blood surrounded a big knot over the man's right eye, and a wider trail of encrusted blood circled around his right cheek and disappeared under his chin. His mouth was partly open. His face was blue and purple, and a small trickle of dried blood showed under his left nostril. His hands were raw and bloody, as were his knees where they had worn through his pants.

The dog also looked in bad shape, but whenever they tried to come close he snarled and showed his teeth. They could see the dog was trying to protect the man. It seemed that movement caused the dog pain. Finally, one hiker took his sleeping bag, threw it over the dog and held him while the other felt for a pulse on the man. Putting his index finger under the man's jaw, he felt a very faint pulse and, while there was no sign of breathing, his body temperature seemed warmer than expected. He tried calling 911, but his cell phone showed "no service."

The hikers were coming off the Appalachian Trail to get supplies at Rucker's Store, which was located where the gravel road intersected with the main road. They pulled the man from the ditch and stretched him out on the ground. The dog kept growling but stayed under the sleeping bag. They decided that one of them would give CPR while the other ran back to get help at a house

1

they had just passed. The hiker took a paper towel and wet it with water from his canteen and wiped off the blood around his mouth and began CPR.

The other hiker ran back to the house for help, and was met by two dogs that wouldn't let him come in the yard. He yelled and, after a few tense moments, a strange apparition appeared at the door. He was a tall man with long, stringy blond hair, wearing a faded feed sack dress and well-worn, high top tennis shoes. The hiker didn't know what to think. The man shushed the dogs but didn't say anything. There was something in his "hush" that made the hiker less fearful. Then, an old woman came out the screen door, drying her hands on her apron, and asked what he wanted. He told them they had found a man nearly dead lying in the ditch. He told her the man had a hound dog lying close beside him.

The woman exclaimed, "Lordy, lordy. Dew, go with this man and see if it's Troop. See if you can help. Mister, we don't have no phone and the woman above this house don't have one neither. The nearest one is just down the road. It's the first house you come to—you can't miss it. Man's name is Clay."

That said, Dew jumped off the porch and loped alongside the hiker. When they got to where the man was lying, Dew's eyes grew big. The hiker could see he was shaking and upset. Dew kneeled down beside Troop and pleaded in a trembling voice, "Troop, what wrong? Troop, wake up."

The hiker who had been giving CPR spoke, "He can't hear you; he's unconscious. Look at that knot on his head. There's another one on the back of his head, too!"

Just then the dog shook off the sleeping bag and looked like he was going to bite the hiker, but Dew spoke, "Blue, Blue, you hurt?"

Blue's posture changed in an instant. He whimpered and tried to crawl to Dew. It was then that they could see his right front leg was broken. There was also a knot with a raw bloody spot on the side of his head.

The hiker giving CPR said he thought he saw shallow breathing, but he wasn't sure. The standing hiker said, "I'm going to run down the road till I get to a house the woman mentioned. She said the man there has a phone. I'll get him to call the rescue squad."

The hiker began running down the road. Breathing heavily, he eventually came to the first driveway and started yelling when he got close enough to be heard. A man came out the back door. His dog headed straight toward the hiker.

"Whoa, Jake! Jake!"

The dog stopped about a yard from the hiker.

"Is your name Clay?"

"Yep."

"There's a man in bad shape just up the road. He has a hound dog this strange guy called Blue. Can you call the rescue squad? If he's not already dead he soon will be."

Clay knew it had to be Troop and Blue.

"I'll make the call, and then we'll ride up there and see if there's anything we can do until they get here."

Clay ran into the house and came back carrying a blanket. While putting on a cap and a light jacket, he motioned for the hiker to get in. Jake jumped in the back of the pickup and Clay spun gravel going down the driveway.

"Wonder what happened?"

"Don't know. Looks like someone tried to kill him. He's beat up bad. We thought he was dead. If he lives, it'll be because that dog laid up against him in those leaves and kept him warm. The dog looks like he got hit in the head, and I think he's got a broken leg."

When Clay got to where Troop was lying, he spoke to Dew and the other hiker. He took the blanket and wrapped it around Troop.

Troop was lying close to the entrance of the road that led to his cabin. Clay wondered who could have done such a thing. To the best of his knowledge Troop didn't have an enemy in the world. He had never heard anyone say anything bad about Troop.

They heard the rescue vehicle coming long before they saw it. After checking him over, the attendants slid him onto a stretcher and put him in the truck; it was then that Clay saw the wound on the back of his head and the matted blood in his hair. They hooked up two IVs—one was a warm saline solution to try to get his core temperature up and the other was a glucose solution.

Dew, who had been standing back and watching, reached down and gently lifted Blue in his arms.

"I take care of Blue. He be okay."

Clay nodded and told the hikers to jump in. He stopped briefly at his house and made Jake get out. Jake never liked being left and showed it as he sulked away.

He dropped off the two hikers at Rucker's Store, thanked them and told them to tell Cecil, the owner, about Troop. "Tell him I'll stop by on the way back from the hospital and let him know his condition."

Clay drove as fast as the law allowed and then some. He knew they would take Troop to the emergency room at Lynchburg General. On the way his thoughts darted from Troop's condition to who could have done it and why.

Troop was a Monacan Indian. Though uneducated in book knowledge, he was smart in ways other people didn't understand. He knew about birds and animals and their habits. He knew tracking—some jokingly said he could track low flying birds. He knew about herbs, plants, healing, and survival. He raised a large garden, kept a milk cow, a flock of chickens and fed out a hog every year. With the exception of salt, sugar, and pepper, he was almost self-sufficient. He canned vegetables from the garden, kept a root cellar for potatoes and had hams, shoulders, side meat, pork chops and sausage from butchering the hog. He hunted ginseng and other roots in the fall. He used his mule, Mabeline, to plow and skid out timber if he needed spending money, which was seldom. He also worked for a few people from time to time, handling cattle, building fences and working in the apple and peach orchards.

As Clay passed T. Wayne Clifton's place, he couldn't help being reminded of the harrowing experience that he, Troop, Sedalia and Robert had with T. Wayne the previous year. There was still a "for sale" sign at the impressive entrance. Someone said his wife was asking around a million. He was formerly a successful trial lawyer in Lynchburg. Currently, he was serving a life sentence for the murder of a local girl.

CHAPTER 2

I've done the calculation and
your chances of winning the lottery are identical
whether you play or not.
—Fran Lebowitz, writer

Clay Hollister had moved back to the family farm near Evergreen in Somerset County in Central Virginia between Lynchburg and Charlottesville. He had taken early retirement from a long career at Merchants and Farmers Bank headquartered in Lynchburg. He was the senior loan officer until the bank sold out to First Citizens in Richmond. His wife had died from cancer a few years back. They had two sons, one in California and the other in North Carolina. He had a small herd of grade Angus cattle, a dog, a cat and a horse. Even though it was lonely at times, he still had friends in Lynchburg along with old and new friends in Evergreen.

He had grown up on the family farm and it had been fairly easy getting assimilated into the community. One of his childhood friends, Robert Tolliver, had also moved back after a career in the army. Robert lived on his old home place along with his wife Corine and his mother, affectionately called "Ant Mabel." Even though Robert and Clay had gone to separate segregated schools, they had been best friends from childhood, playing kids' games, going fishing, and playing baseball. They played baseball at every opportunity.

Troop had previously entered the picture when "Dewberry" Jones was arrested for the murder of an attractive local girl, Sally Jessup. Dew was the man who went with the hiker to help Troop.

Sally was well-liked and popular in the community, especially with the men. She had lived with her mother Thelma at the end of Spruce Creek Road. Dew and his mother Gladys lived just below Thelma and Sally. After the murder, the sheriff arrested Dew, claiming he found Dew's knife in Little Spruce Creek. He said he saw the sun dancing off the open blade in the creek after it receded from an early spring rain. He said the knife was the murder weapon. Troop was one of the few who could carry on a conversation with Dew.

These thoughts and past memories were racing through Clay's head when he pulled into the emergency room parking lot at Lynchburg General Hospital.

Clay saw one of the rescue squad members standing outside on the dock. He recognized him, but didn't know his name. He was holding a cigarette in his left hand, with his right hand in his pocket and staring at the floor, looking dejected. When Clay approached, he looked up and shook his head slowly.

"I don't know. If he lives, it'll be a miracle. He flatlined twice on the way. I kept doing CPR. Thank goodness for that "fibulator." I got him jump-started, but it don't look good."

Clay asked the harried receptionist if he could go back and check on Troop. She seemed more interested in getting information about Troop's nearest relatives and if he had health insurance. Clay explained he was just a neighbor and didn't know anything about his relatives or if he had insurance. She finally let Clay go back in the patient area of the ER. Cubicles were separated by curtains around each bed with just enough room for the patient and doctors and nurses. There was a doctor hovering over Troop, working on his wounds. A nurse was helping, checking his pulse and watching his heart monitor. Troop's breathing seemed labored.

The doctor acknowledged Clay, speaking and examining at the same time. "It's a miracle he's alive, but he looks in good physical condition. Most of the people we see are overweight and out of shape."

The heavyset nurse glared at the doctor. The doctor said they were going to do some x-rays, an MRI, and some other tests and told Clay to have a seat in the waiting area and to check back in about an hour.

Clay went back to the waiting area and searched for a magazine or newspaper. CNN was on the TV, but the volume was too low to hear and the closed caption was too small to read. He realized he was continuing to think about Troop and Dew and the previous year's events and was too preoccupied to watch TV or read.

Dew was an oddity in the community that locals took for granted. He had several older sisters who had grown up and moved away. People said Dew's mother Gladys held him back because she thought he was a little slow. They said that early on she dressed him in his sisters' hand-me-downs. The only problem was that Dew never made the transition to men's clothes. Gladys continued to make plain dresses for Dew from feed sacks, which he wore with high top tennis shoes. They lived in a remote part of the county so they seldom saw other people. Dew walked down Spruce Creek Road once a week to get groceries at Rucker's Store. Cecil Rucker, the owner, charged the weekly bills, which Gladys paid every month with her Social Security check. Dew could speak and answer basic questions with short simple answers. He just looked strange to outsiders. At 6'4", with stringy blond hair, a peach fuzz beard, and hairy legs sticking out from under the feed sack dress, he caused strangers to do a double take. Shy and withdrawn, Dew would nod if spoken to and give a crooked grin and a waist high hand wave.

Thinking back to Dew's arrest, the locals at Rucker's had talked daily about how unlikely it was for Dew to hurt anyone, but the sheriff had strong evidence with the knife. The day after he was arrested, Clay and Robert were talking at Rucker's about Dew when

Troop approached and asked Robert if he would take him to the county jail at Lynhurst to visit Dew. Robert said he was headed out of town the next day, but Clay, who knew Troop, told him he was going to Lynhurst and would be glad to give him a ride.

On the ride that day, Troop talked about Dew. He said, "Dew got plenty good sense. He 'hopes' me round the farm and he can talk okay when he wants to."

Clay asked Troop if he could sit in on the jail visit if he kept quiet and sat a little behind him. Troop said he reckoned that would be all right.

When the deputy brought Dew in, he looked frightened, disheveled and disoriented. Clay's heart went out to him and he felt a lump in his throat. Dew kept asking "home, home?" Troop told him he couldn't go home today and asked if he hurt Sally.

"No hurt Sally, like Sally. Sally good to Dew."

When Troop asked Dew about the sheriff finding his knife, he twisted and turned and looked like he didn't know what to say. But while squirming and turning, Dew caught sight of the sheriff in the background talking to some jail employees. Looking toward the sheriff, Dew blurted out, "Him took, him took!"

Neither Clay nor Troop could believe what they heard. Why would the sheriff take his knife and arrest Dew? On the way home they concluded that Dew was being set up, or made a "patsy" for some kind of cover-up. They also realized they had to keep quiet about what they heard and be careful about how to proceed. Clay suggested they tell Robert because he did some kind of police work in the army. In retirement, he sometimes consulted with companies setting up security systems. Troop agreed and suggested they also include Sedalia.

Clay was puzzled as to why Troop suggested Sedalia. Troop made some equally confusing comments about Sedalia being like a medicine man, that she had the gift—that she saw things; that sometimes she knew things before they happened; and that she could talk to animals.

Clay had met Sedalia after a small screech owl had collided with the window of his car. Clay was driving back from Lynchburg that night. He turned around and went back and found the little owl in a daze sitting on the white line. The next morning he took the owl to Sedalia because he had heard she worked with birds that were wounded or sick. The only thing anyone in the Evergreen community knew about her was that she had moved here from somewhere out west. Someone said she had lived in one of those four corner states. She was friendly but reclusive and seemed detached. She didn't get involved in community activities or go out of her way to meet people. Her appearance reminded him of the country singer, Emmy Lou Harris. She seemed contented looking after her dogs, geese, ducks and a few head of beef cattle.

Clay remembered that first visit. It seemed she barely noticed him after she saw the owl. She took the bird, hardly said a word, and walked away. He left feeling like the ugliest puppy at the dog pound.

CHAPTER 3

Early to bed and early to rise
probably indicates unskilled labor.
—John Ciardi

In the waiting room Clay saw various looks of concern and heard noisy chatter. Some appeared lost in their own thoughts. Others looked like they were there just to see what was going on. It always bothered Clay that some people used the emergency room for things better handled in a doctor's office or the free clinic. It didn't seem right to tie up doctors and nurses for minor ailments when people with more serious conditions were waiting.

Continuing to reflect on their earlier experience, Clay was glad Troop suggested Sedalia because, as the group worked through Dew's ordeal, he had grown very close to her. When the group met, it was uncanny how their talents blended. They all agreed on Dew's innocence. They wondered why Dew was being set up and what they could do about it.

At their first meeting, Troop related that one night when he came in from coon hunting, he saw T. Wayne's Mercedes parked in the turnout at the high bridge on Little Spruce Creek. He was sure there was a woman with him. The bridge was just above the place in the creek where Sally's body was found.

Robert gave his take on what he believed happened. He said that since Sally had stab wounds and broken bones, she had probably been beaten, stabbed and thrown off the high bridge onto the rocks below. The swollen waters of Little Spruce Creek took her into an elbow of the creek under a cliff where her body lodged in a logjam. Sedalia added that it didn't make sense for the sheriff to arrest Dew and asked if the sheriff was somehow tied in with Sally's death. She suggested that each one think about what they knew, make some discrete inquiries and get back together later.

At the second meeting Troop said he talked with Sally's mother Thelma. She told him Sally was seeing some rich man, but she didn't know who. Troop also said he had recently seen familiar tire tracks at the turnout and figured T. Wayne had been up there in his Mercedes.

Clay had visited an old high school friend who owned the local funeral home. Bernard told him he handled Sally's funeral and the knife wounds were deeper than any blade on a regular pocketknife. He also said the autopsy would show the depth of the stab wounds: that is, if anyone bothered to study the autopsy and compare the blade length. They feared Dew wouldn't get a trial and that he would be judged incompetent and be put in a state mental facility for life.

Since it had been about an hour, Clay decided to go back to see if there was any news about Troop. A nurse told him he was in a coma, that he was still being monitored and there were other tests they needed to do. She said she would come out and tell him as soon as she knew something.

Clay returned to the waiting room and flipped aimlessly through a magazine, but his thoughts went back to Dew's ordeal. The group considered why T. Wayne's distinctive tire tracks, like Michelins, showed up after the murder. They thought perhaps he was looking for the murder weapon. It had been Troop who suggested they get a man he knew in Buena Vista to bring his bloodhound over to see what he would find.

Clay asked Hazel, a waitress at Raeford's, to try to save something of T. Wayne's the next time he came in for lunch. He had lunch frequently with his sidekick, Lennie. It was known that T. Wayne and Lennie often bought foreclosed property the county and lenders auctioned off. Clay suggested a napkin, a cigarette butt, gum wrapper—whatever. Hazel saved not only his napkin and cigarette pack and butts; she also got one of T. Wayne's leather gloves from his coat pocket. Clay knew Hazel and asked her to keep it confidential. He promised he would explain later. Hazel disliked T. Wayne because he made a mess, was arrogant, and left a small tip.

The group doubted if the bloodhound would find anything because it had been over two weeks since the murder. Oddly enough, the bloodhound struck a trail on the path along the west side of Little Spruce Creek, but the trail went cold and nothing was found. They believed finding any trail meant that T. Wayne had been up the path since the murder.

While they were standing around thanking the man for bringing his dog, a black Ford pickup truck with dark tinted windows came roaring up Spruce Creek Road. The driver hit his brakes, did a slick 180 like a moonshine driver and fishtailed back down the road. They speculated as to what that was all about and worried that T. Wayne or the sheriff, or both, were watching them. Clay told Sedalia later that Hazel was going to put the glove back in T. Wayne's coat pocket the next time he came in. They laughed, wondering what T. Wayne would think when his lost glove suddenly reappeared.

At about the same time two hunters from Charlottesville made what seemed like an unrelated discovery. While spring gobbler hunting on the abandoned Wheeler place, they stopped to get a drink of water from the old well. When they pulled up the old tin bucket, it contained a partially decomposed fetus. They took it back in their plastic lunch bag to Rucker's store. They were going to call the sheriff but luckily a Virginia State Trooper had stopped for lunch so they turned it over to him. The group wondered if Sally had gotten pregnant and had a miscarriage or an abortion. They thought maybe she told T. Wayne that she was pregnant and was threatening blackmail. The group began to believe Dew's arrest had to be a cover-up that involved the sheriff and T. Wayne.

CHAPTER 4

Church Sign:
If you're looking for a sign from God, this is it!
Sunday morning 11:00 a.m.

Back in the ER, the doctor broke his train of thought. He looked somber. He said Troop had a severe concussion and was in a coma. They didn't know if there was brain damage or when, or if, he would regain consciousness. He said Troop had been put in the intensive care unit and suggested that Clay go home and call the hospital periodically for updates on Troop's condition. He decided to go home and call Sedalia and Robert.

Clay left instructions to call him if Troop's condition worsened. By then it was well past noon and he was hungry so he decided to stop by Raeford's Restaurant just outside Lynhurst on Route 29. Raeford's was a favorite local eatery where blue collar, white collar, and no collar ate. It was a common scene to see a BMW or a Lexus parked beside a load of hay or timber, or a Harley. Professionals, laborers, local police, office workers, truck drivers, retirees, farmers, tradesmen, real estate agents, and college professors were in the mix. If you looked under the tables or at the feet of those sitting at the counter, you would see muddy work boots, sneakers, sandals, loafers, high heels and flip-flops. Some of the best dressed with the fanciest cars had the least money and some with older vehicles and the worst dressed were millionaires. Clay always saw someone he knew and Raeford good-naturedly insulted all his best customers.

Jokingly, with everyone listening, he yelled at Clay, "Does your parole officer know where you are?" Raeford then asked one of his typical inane questions, "Don't you think Viagra ought to be classified as a performance enhancing drug?"

Clay laughed and responded, "I don't know. You may be better qualified to answer that than me. By the way, do you think boot camp and rat year at military schools is bullying?"

Raeford laughed and said, "Touché."

As usual, Clay sat at the counter and Doris took his order. He was particularly hungry so he ordered salmon cakes, applesauce, coleslaw, homemade rolls and unsweetened iced tea. Doris always stuck three lemon slices on the glass rim.

Eli, the well-known womanizer, was also sitting at the counter. He was on his right with one seat between them and, as usual, he was trying to hit on Doris.

"Doris, darlin', you're lookin' a little under the weather. Are you feelin' okay?"

"No, not really. I think I might have a little fever."

"I shore would like to take your temperature."

Doris twisted up her mouth and put the evil eye on Eli and said, "I don't think your thermometer is capable of giving me a good reading, Eli."

As she walked away, the next guy over laughed and slapped his knee and exclaimed, "Damn, Eli, she got you again; ain't you never gonna learn?"

Eli gave a sheepish grin.

There wasn't much time for reflection after leaving Raeford's since it took only about fifteen minutes to get to Rucker's store. While Raeford's was one of the best places to eat and hear what was going on in and around the county seat, Rucker's was the community center and the best place to learn all the news around Evergreen. The store was a combination grocery, gas, feed, hardware and deli. Cecil Rucker, the owner, played music to suit his taste, which ranged from old time country and bluegrass to rock and roll, blues, classical and even opera, but only the tenors. He knew everyone and everything going on in Evergreen. He, his father, and grandfather had run a store in the same location for well over a hundred years. You could buy horse, cattle, hog and chicken feed as well as seeds, tablecloth, kitchen linoleum, wood stoves, and chewing tobacco. Also, he carried bolts and nails, a large round of old sharp Cheddar cheese, snuff, cigarette papers to roll your own, and rings to put in pigs' noses to keep them from rooting. There were also work shoes and clothes, fertilizer and a barrel of salt fish in brine. Cecil was also the Evergreen postmaster.

There was usually a group of locals gathered around an old potbellied wood stove that had been brought over to the new store twenty years ago after Cecil outgrew the old building. Cecil never put a fire in it. It was the centerpiece for the locals to gather around to eat, drink coffee, and talk. When Clay walked in, those congregated were anxious to hear about Troop's condition. The core group included Woodrow Cremmins, the now rich sawmill owner and land baron who had bought timberland over the years, cut the timber and kept the land; "Bull," the dump truck driver whose voice sounded like a bull frog and was built like a fire plug; Bill Ware, the owner of a garage across from Rucker's; and Burl, the almost permanent fixture who delighted in telling tall tales. Burl served as the clearinghouse for all news, rumor and gossip in Evergreen. Cecil also came over to find out about Troop. There were others in the community who felt free to drift in and out of the conversations including Walter, a retired farmer, who had an unfortunate stammer.

Clay told them that Troop was in real bad shape. He told them the doctor said it looked like someone hit him in the back of the head, causing him to fall forward, hitting his forehead, probably on a rock. He told them the doctor said if he regained consciousness he could easily have memory loss or even brain damage.

The conversation meandered from who could have done it, or why. Bill Ware and Bull had gone up to Troop's cabin to check on things and said there was no sign that anything had been disturbed. They felt robbery was not a motive and that the beating did not take place at the cabin. The conclusion was that he must have been beaten away from the cabin and had somehow struggled to get to Spruce Creek Road for help before he passed out.

While they were talking, others had joined the circle. Then, for the first time, Clay noticed the tall, gaunt man staring at him. He was leaning against a grocery shelf close enough to hear but far enough back to be overlooked. His deep-set, cold, dark eyes never blinked. Clay averted his own eyes, but when he looked again, the man was still glaring. His elongated face, hawkish nose and long black beard added to his sinister appearance. Clay didn't think he had ever seen him before. He was broad shouldered, lanky, and stood over six feet. He wore dirty overalls and a sweat stained khaki shirt with frayed cuffs and collar. Clay looked away again. When he glanced back the man was still staring—the penetrating cold eyes never wavered. He felt a shiver go up his spine. The eyes were evil, like the man could see into his very soul. Clay glanced away again. When he looked back, the man was leaving. He was putting on a worn floppy black felt hat as he went out the door.

As the group dispersed, Clay cornered Cecil and asked about the stranger. Cecil said his name was Easel and he was Ole Devil Rip's brother. Clay felt embarrassed because Cecil said it in such a way that he thought he should know Ole Devil Rip.

Cecil also seemed puzzled. He said, "Ole Rip's clan is about fifteen miles away in Nelson County and is about as far back in the mountains as you can get. On the other hand, Ole Rip's land curves back toward Evergreen on the other side of the mountain and isn't more than four or five miles away as the crow flies. You would have to hike around Big Mount Bishop and a couple of high ridges to get there."

Clay picked up on the tone of Cecil's answer. "You sound like you don't think much of Ole Rip."

"That's putting it mildly. He and his bunch are bad news. He supposedly cuts timber for a living, but the rumor is he makes most of his money from moonshine."

Clay asked, "Wonder what he was doin' over in this neck of the woods? And did you notice the awful smell over there where he was standing? It smelled rancid and rotten."

Cecil continued. "Beats me. I've only seen that one in here once or twice in my life. Ole Rip used to come in occasionally, but I haven't seen him for years. And yeah, I did smell something. Did you notice he had a fresh bandage on his left hand?"

"No, I didn't. That name Rip does ring a bell. Seems like my father used to buy locust posts for fencing from a man named Rip."

"That's probably him. He used to be halfway decent, but I've heard he's gotten meaner with age. And he's got two sons that are literally hell on wheels. They both keep new four-wheel-drive Ford 350 diesel dually pickups*. If they've been drinkin', which is often, you damn sure better let them have the road. If you want to hear some hell raisin' stories, just ask Jessie Brown."

Clay knew Jessie was a county deputy who lived in the community.

"That guy looked at me like he could cut my throat."

"And he probably would, too. He looks at everyone the same way."

With that, Clay bought a few groceries and left.

---

* A dually pickup is a heavy-duty pickup with two extra wheels on the rear axle, often used to pull trailers and equipment.

CHAPTER 5

I stopped believing in Santa Claus when I was six.
My mother took me to see him in a department store
and he asked me for my autograph.
—Shirley Temple

On the way home, Clay's thoughts flitted back and forth from the strange man to Sedalia and Robert. He needed to call them about Troop. In spite of the bad news, he looked forward to talking with Sedalia. She seemed to welcome his calls, but he always felt less obvious if he had something of interest to relate.

When Sedalia answered the phone, Clay asked her if she had heard about Troop and she said, "What about Troop?"

"He's in bad shape. Two hikers found him this morning lying in the ditch next to his road entrance. He was almost dead. Somebody really did a number on him. He's in a coma in Lynchburg General. The doctor said he didn't know when, or if, he'd come out of it."

"That's awful—it hasn't been that long since he got burned in that barn fire, and now this."

"I know, and whoever hit Troop also beat up Blue pretty bad. Dew has him. I thought I'd go up tomorrow morning and take him to the vet. I don't know why, but Blue has never liked me. Would you consider riding along?"

"Sure, what time?"

"Is ten o'clock okay?"

"See you then."

Clay called Robert and filled him in on Troop's condition.

"Why are all these things happening to us?" asked Robert.

"What do you mean?"

"I'm sure I don't have to remind you of all the stuff we went through back when they arrested Dew."

"I see what you mean."

"My gut tells me this is something the police are not going to solve unless Troop regains consciousness and remembers who did it."

"I see where you're headed. Do you think we need to call a meeting of the Ginseng Gang?"

"Tell you what. Sedalia and I are going to take Blue to the vet tomorrow; I'll ask her."

"Hell, Clay, she can probably go into a trance and tell you who did it."

"Now Robert."

"Just kidding, you know I like Sedalia, but sometimes she scares me with her intuition, or whatever."

"I'll let you know."

"Talk to you later."

When Clay picked up Sedalia, she started right away.

"If robbery wasn't the motive and it didn't happen at his cabin, it must have happened somewhere in the woods. If it had happened at the cabin, Troop's other dogs, Buckshot and Ruby, would have helped protect him. The puzzle is how he got from where he was beaten to the side of the road."

"Maybe the person, or persons, that beat him knocked him out and dragged him to the road, or maybe he crawled or staggered to the road before he passed out," responded Clay.

"Maybe they didn't want to kill him. Maybe they just wanted to teach him a lesson."

"It was a hell of a lesson! Looks like they didn't care if he remembered it."

As they turned into the driveway, they saw Dew sitting on the floor of the front porch with his hairy legs dangling down. Blue was lying in a cardboard box beside him. Dew gave a grin and a half wave.

Sedalia walked up and rubbed Blue—it looked like he leaned his head into her hand. Clay knew to stand back. She slowly leaned over and examined Blue. Dew and Gladys had cleaned his head wound and put some ointment on the cut. When she touched his leg, he winced and whimpered.

Sedalia spoke to Dew and Gladys. "We need to take him to get his leg fixed. We'll bring him back and bring some food for you to feed him." Dew nodded. Sedalia told Gladys about Troop's condition. "Will you take care of him till Troop gets better?"

"Be glad to. Lordy, lordy, what's this world comin' to? Reckon somebody ought to feed his other dogs and chickens."

"That's right," replied Sedalia.

Turning to Clay, she asked, "Does it suit you to go by and check on things after we get back?"

"I was thinking the same thing."

CHAPTER 6

Saying:

You would think by now they would have found
something closer to godliness than cleanliness.

Clay knew to take Blue to Henrietta. She was the only vet close by. Her office was just outside Lynhurst. She was a strong-willed, firm-jawed woman who preferred horses and cattle to small dogs and cats, but she could do it all. She was a "no-nonsense, get to it, and do it" type. Most people who knew her called her "Henry," which she seemed to prefer. It wasn't that she was masculine; it was more that she wasn't feminine. Some speculated that she might be a lesbian, but no one knew or cared. She was friends with Sedalia and visited her occasionally, which caused some of the same gossipy types to speculate about Sedalia.

Dew lifted Blue and laid him across Sedalia's lap. She cradled his head and rubbed his neck and ears and talked to him. He didn't seem to mind that his hindquarters covered the middle of the seat and rested against Clay's leg.

Sedalia had to carry Blue into Henry's office and place him on the stainless steel table. He growled at the attendant. Sedalia talked softly to him while Henry gave him a sedative. As soon as he was asleep, she x-rayed the leg. After studying the x-ray, she cut the skin from the elbow to the knee and examined the break. She commented that luckily it was a clean, straight-across break. Henry opened up the skin around the break and then she screwed on a plate and sutured the wound. She examined the knot on his head and gave Blue an antibiotic and gave Sedalia some ointment to rub on the wound. She said if he got along okay to bring him back in a couple of weeks and she would check him over and remove the stitches.

Clay carried the still-sedated Blue to the pickup and put him in Sedalia's lap. On the way home Clay related Robert's suggestion that it might be a good idea to call a meeting of the Ginseng Gang and discuss what the three thought about what happened to Troop. Sedalia agreed, but questioned if anyone knew enough to have any ideas at this stage.

Upon arriving at the home of Dew and Gladys, Clay laid Blue on the blanket in the box. He began waking and although still groggy, he gave a half-hearted growl when he recognized Clay. Sedalia told Dew and Gladys that Blue might need some help when he tried to stand. Clay left a bag of dog food that he had picked up at Rucker's. He had also bought another bag of dog food to take for Troop's other dogs.

After leaving Dew and Gladys, Clay and Sedalia went to Troop's place. He put the truck in four-wheel drive and drove up the steep, rutted road to Troop's cabin. Ruby, a redbone bitch, and Buckshot, a black and tan hound, met them with tails wagging. Unlike Blue, Ruby and Buckshot liked Clay.

"I feel like an intruder going in here."

"Me, too," responded Clay, "but we don't have a choice. I doubt if Troop ever bought dog food. He probably fed them leftovers from what he ate—cornbread and scraps. Troop used to say, 'Hit takes a lean hound for a long chase.'"

"Whatever it was, they look lean and healthy."

Sedalia poured some dry food in the pan. Ruby watched as Buckshot smelled it and took a bite. Then Ruby joined in.

Clay added, "Hounds aren't too hard to please. Besides, I expect Bull and Bill gave them something when they came up."

After feeding the dogs, they went to the barn. Mabeline, the mule, came up to the fence and stuck her nose over the top. Troop was as close to Mabeline as he was to Blue. Clay gave her some hay. Sedalia found a bag of cracked corn and put some in the bucket for the chickens. The flock was scratching around the yard and in front of the chicken house. They came running and dove in when she scattered it on the ground. She went inside and gathered ten brown eggs from the nests.

They saw Millie, his Guernsey milk cow, and gave her some hay.

"I wonder if she needs milking?" asked Sedalia.

"No, she's bred, but not due for a month or two."

Looking at the beehive, Sedalia asked about the bees.

"I don't know. I'll ask at Rucker's if anyone knows about bees. Sometimes you have to feed them sugar water in the spring, but I'm not sure about fall and winter. Knowing Troop, I'm sure he left enough honey to get them through the winter."

On the way to Sedalia's house, Clay said, "I'm sure it's going to be awhile before Troop recovers. In the meantime, I guess I'll try to keep a watch on things. I don't think he has any family—not close-by anyway."

"I'll be happy to help—just give me a call."

"Thanks. Let's keep each other posted if either hears any news."

CHAPTER 7

Church Sign:
Don't make me have to come down there. GOD

Clay wanted to get to Rucker's that morning before nine, knowing the coffee club would be there and he could ask for advice about the bees. When he walked in, he saw the group huddled in a deep discussion. They didn't even look up. Clay poured and fixed his coffee and walked over. Nods were exchanged, but the intense discussion continued.

Burl was speaking. "If you ask me, it won't no accident. Mack was a careful driver and he took good care of his equipment. My guess is that damn bunch of rednecks were drag racing on that stretch before you get to the bridge and the curve. I'll bet you ten to one when Mack came around that curve, two of those drag racers were in a side by side dead heat and Mack swerved to miss'em. With a heavy load of logs, the side of the road either gave way or the high center of gravity of the load caused him to lose control and hit that bridge abutment. The load could have also shifted when he swerved so there won't no way he coulda brought it back. I'll guarandam tee ya that one of them boys was Junior Dooley. He's 'bout as worthless as tits on a bo' hog. His mama ruined him and his daddy's too chicken to stand up to either one of 'em. If his daddy won't doin' so well in the truckin' business, Junior wouldn't be able to mess around with buildin' hot rods and drag racin'."

Clay sat down on a low, wooden, slat-bottom chair and cradled his coffee between his hands. Woodrow spoke to Clay. "We just heard Mack Hanes got killed. He wrecked in the curve before the straight stretch on the road to Afton late yesterday afternoon.

One of the rescue squad men told Bull he was so mangled they had to put him in a body bag. Mack rammed the bridge abutment head on and then flipped over. They said the cab crumpled like an accordion with all that weight behind it. Burl thinks a couple of drag racers might have caused it, and he might be right. There ain't no skid marks 'cept where Mack ran off the road. The state trooper said none of Mack's tires had blown and he doubted Mack had a heart attack."

All Clay could say was, "Damn, someone has got to do something about these crazy drivers! What a waste!"

About that time Robert came in and Clay asked if he had heard.

"Yeah, I heard. This might do Lula in. Her health ain't too good, and she and Mack were mighty close. Corine, Mama and I are going to see her this afternoon. I've known Mack all my life. We go to the same church. There's somethin' funny 'bout this whole thing."

"That's what everybody here thinks, too. Guess I better call Sedalia. What with Troop and now this, I hope that saying about bad things happening in threes is wrong!"

Clay got some sliced roast beef and cereal and headed home. When he reached Sedalia's she was incredulous. "What next! This is so sad. I'll fix something and take it by this afternoon. I've heard Lula is very religious, but I don't know if she'll be able to handle this."

"You mind if I come along? I was close to Mack. He was the one I had 'select' cut the timber on the mountain section last year and he did a great job. I never worried about Mack doing anything crooked like some loggers do. He only cut the ones that needed it and he didn't make a mess. I'll get something to take, too. With the funeral arrangements and all the children and people coming, Lula will have her hands full. How about I pick you up 'round four?"

"Sounds good. See you then."

Clay thought about what to get and decided to go to the bakery in Lynhurst and get a couple of pies and then pick up a bucket of Kentucky fried chicken. The drive to and from town was like most drives for Clay—it gave him a chance to think about all that had happened, along with other unrelated things that came to mind. Would he, Robert and Sedalia be able to figure out what happened to Troop? If Troop recovered, would he remember who attacked him? The nurse said something about amnesia. If the law can't catch all these dangerous drivers, could the group figure out something? He wondered what Robert learned in the army in the CID. In the past, Robert had dropped a few hints about investigations, surveillance, gathering evidence, and forensic analysis.

On the way back he stopped at Raeford's. The place was crowded. The food was good, the service was excellent, the prices were reasonable and it was always a treat to be insulted by Raeford. When he walked in the door he caught Raeford's eye. He yelled at Clay, "You getting back from an AA meeting? Aren't you still on work release?"

Clay sat at the counter and picked up the small, single mimeographed menu. The menus were different each day of the week, but were the same for that day all the time. Raeford would put a little humor sometimes on the border. Today's quote was "Pie are not square. Pie are round. Cornbread are square," which most of his customers didn't understand unless they had taken geometry.

Clay ordered one of his favorite lunches—stewed tomatoes, black-eyed peas, coleslaw and cornbread muffins. He told Doris he wanted his usual water with a couple of slices of lemon. He squeezed the lemon slices and stirred the water. He rubbed the excess lemon juice on his hands. He knew lemon juice was probably as good as any antibacterial soap and it smelled better. The guy next to him got the house salad piled high with chopped onions plus potato salad and saltines. The guy on the other side got a chuck wagon steak and covered it with Texas Pete.

When he got home he got the mail out of the mailbox and was greeted by Jake when he reached the house. Jake was his pound rescued lab-Rottweiler plus other descendants of unknown heritage. As an old judge once remarked about one of his frequent court attendees, "He couldn't even trace his ancestry on his mother's side."

Rita, his cat, observed with arrogant disdain Jake's shameless groveling and submissiveness. Rita decided when she wanted to be affectionate and she was never on call just because Clay had been away for a while. She made the choice as to when and where affection would be permitted. Bill Ware once said there was no need to name a cat 'cause they only come when they want to.

By the time he had read his mail, checked for messages, taken a shower and dressed, there was still a little time left. He sat for a few moments and Rita jumped in his lap. She did the pumping thing against his thigh that cats do and then curled up in his lap. Clay rubbed the back of her neck and thought about Sedalia. He had to admit he thought of her often. He had steadily felt closer to her as they worked together to help Dew when he was falsely arrested for murder. He felt sure she enjoyed his company but there were few signs of affection other than friendship. Clay knew enough not to push it and even he had a difficult time figuring how far he wanted to take the relationship. Oh well, friendship was good enough for now. Still, he wondered about her past—if she had been married, jilted, or abused, or maybe still in love with someone else. She never mentioned any friends calling, writing, or coming to visit. He could have imagined her detachment and indifference if it weren't for her obvious love of animals and her deep concern for Troop and Mack's wife. She did say she had training as a wildlife rehabilitator for birds, especially hawks. Troop said she could get inside animals' heads and communicate with them. That seemed a bit of a stretch, but Clay knew people who could gentle disturbed animals. Most of their bad habits were the result of something that had been done to them. If you could figure out what it was, you could work with them to overcome it and rebuild their trust and confidence. He hoped he would learn more about Sedalia and if she had any old wounds, distrust, or other problems.

When he pulled into her yard, the ducks and even the geese came running. It was always a rush of animals. The dogs welcomed and the ducks hoped for a handout, but he would always watch the geese. The old gander was unpredictable and fearless. He never turned his back on the gander. Geese are better guard animals than most dogs. You don't know fear until you've been charged by a large gander with his neck extended, his wings arched and fully raised, like the "touchdown" signal, hissing and squawking. Their bite can leave a serious bruise on your buttocks. They will take on all comers regardless of size. The only one they respected was Sedalia. Clay saw the bags on the front porch and heard Sedalia coming down the steps inside.

She greeted Clay warmly. "How's it going? Heard anything new on Troop?"

"I called last night. He's still in intensive care, but stable."

"I called this morning and they said the same thing. I'm hopeful; we can't afford to lose Troop—he's special."

"I know," Clay replied, "he's kind and generous and would help anyone anyway he could for as long as it took, and he'd be upset if you tried to pay him."

"He's a good soul and smart. He knows things he can't even explain how he knows. By the way, what did you find out about the bees?"

"I forgot to ask, what with Mack and all. I'll ask the next time I see anyone who knows about bees. I know beekeeping isn't simple. The inner-workings of a hive are complicated. There are drones, workers, and the queen. I've heard the drones are only there to fertilize the queen, and the mating process kills the drones. They say they just explode."

"Hmm," mused Sedalia.

Clay continued, "I can almost see the workers having committee meetings. The workers know when the queen is wearing out and how and when to raise a new one. She has her own attendants who feed her and look after her every need. Queens often live up to five years, but the average bee only lives six to eight weeks in the prime honey season. They literally work themselves to death."

"Sounds like you know a little something about bees."

"I don't know anything about judging the food supply. I've heard about beehives and country people keeping bees for as long as I can remember. I've thought about getting my own hive, but it's not simple. I remember hearing about a beekeeper in Bedford County who had over twenty hives, but one year the bears nearly wiped him out, so he dropped back to just a few hives, mainly for his own use. There are other pests, too, like skunks, mice and mites. And there's another problem called colony collapse disorder that can kill off an entire hive. Anyway, I'll try to remember to ask the next time I see the group at Rucker's. By the way, one of the most interesting things made from honey is mead. It's the oldest fermented drink in the world."

CHAPTER 8

Always go to other peoples' funerals;
otherwise, they won't come to yours.

—(supposedly) Yogi Berra

They could see the cars and pickups lining both sides of the road near the entrance to Mack and Lula's home. The one and a half story bungalow with dormer windows and dark green shutters had a red tin roof that overhung the full-length front porch. The house was in the center of a well-kept yard with trees, shrubbery and Lula's flower gardens. It sat back about two hundred feet from the state maintained gravel road.

"I don't know much about funeral customs in these parts. You think it's okay for us to go in?"

"Sure. Among the long-time local people around here, you might see as many of one race as the other, especially if the person who died was well liked. At a black people's church most of the white people will sit toward the back, but with Mack, there'll be so many you sit anywhere you can find a seat. The same is generally reversed in a white church. Everybody liked Mack so you are going to see the whole community grieve.

Clay carried Sedalia's bags and could feel the weight of how much she had prepared. They went around the side of the house to the back door. The weather had warmed somewhat and a group of men were sitting and standing around a picnic table. Others stood in small groups, talking quietly. Clay knew or recognized most of the men, both black and white, and they nodded to each other. Corine, Robert's wife, welcomed them and opened the back door to let them in. Sedalia had never seen so much food. The kitchen table was full of plates, bowls, and other dishes. All the counter space was full of the same. The cakes, pies, and other desserts were on the table on the enclosed back porch. Food seemed to be one of the best ways people had to express their condolences.

Sedalia was surprised at how easy it was to mingle and join different groups that were remembering Mack and speculating as to what had caused the wreck. The women of Mack and Lula's church were taking care of things as they also would on the day of the funeral.

Clay heard more diverse conversations about not having seen each other for so long and that people didn't get together like they used to and that other than at the grocery store, funerals and church, they didn't see each other as they did in earlier times.

It wasn't necessary to stay long so Clay and Sedalia said their goodbyes and left. Clay told Sedalia that since the funeral was day after tomorrow at one o'clock, they had better get there before 12:30 if they wanted to get a seat.

CHAPTER 9

Church Sign:
God is too big to fit inside one religion.

The morning before the funeral, Clay decided to walk through the upper pasture behind the house and the barn. Before entering the woods, he stopped to catch his breath and take in the panoramic view of the mountains and valleys. Large white clouds were moving fast in the upper atmosphere. He watched the resulting shadows on the ridges that were interspersed with areas of bright sunshine and brilliant colors. The fall sun illuminated the reds, greens, yellows and oranges. In a few weeks most of the leaves would be gone, leaving the mountains naked and open, except for the scattered pines, evergreens and thickets.

Clay smiled as he thought about Burl telling newcomers and folks from the city about all of nature's signals of weather changes. He'd say that if wooly worms had a lot of dark it meant a cold winter and if the dark ring was around their head it meant an early snow. He'd tell them a lot of acorns meant a hard winter and that the number of foggy mornings in August foretold the number of snows to expect. He also said that when a cat slept with its paws underneath her, you could expect bad weather. Clay knew these weren't accurate, but they made a good story.

He also knew there were some signs you could count on like the old saying of red sky at night—sailors delight and red sky in the morning—sailor take warning. A halo around the moon means rain or snow is coming. Lots of birds at your feeder can mean bad weather is on the way. The saying "clear moon-frost soon" was reliable. Green clouds can mean a tornado and any strange color like yellow is a bad sign. They say cattle lie down before a rain and stuck windows and clogged salt shakers mean a storm is coming.

Entering the woods from the pasture, he walked along the wood road. Walking allowed the mind to wander, relax, and contemplate. Overhead he saw a red tail hawk and heard its "eeee" call. He thought about Troop. The hospital said all the vital signs were now stable, but he was still in a coma. He thought about Mack and the agony Lula was going through and the loneliness to come and whether she would want to stay on in the house by herself. Maybe she would give in and move to town to live with one of her children. He wondered if she would die in a year or two as often happens when a couple was as close as she and Mack.

Clay thought back to Sally's murder and how the Ginseng Gang had concluded that T. Wayne had to be the murderer. The odd behavior of the pickup driver the day they used the bloodhound made them believe they were being watched. Clay had done more checking in the clerk's office and found that the sheriff and T. Wayne were the two main shareholders in a real estate investment corporation. Troop had seen fresh tire marks at the turnout above the bridge that seemed to match T. Wayne's Mercedes. The bloodhound picking up T. Wayne's scent made them wonder if T. Wayne had been back looking for something. The clincher came when Clay found a note in his mailbox written with a crayon that said, "We want what you found. Put it in the mailbox at the old Wheeler place by midnight Saturday or else." They deduced the pickup driver had seen them holding the paper bag with the scent items and assumed they had found the murder weapon. It meant the weapon was still in the woods. Why else had T. Wayne been returning to the scene? Clay went to Lynchburg and rented three metal detectors. The group then laid out a grid and methodically covered the area along Little Spruce Creek. They assigned squares and marked off each area covered. The metal detectors picked up beer, sardine and pork and bean cans that fishermen had discarded.

They all heard the loud beeps when Sedalia's detector found the knife. The upscale label on the knife showed the brand name and it was likely from a set.

When Clay got back to the house it was time to get ready and pick up Sedalia. He dressed in one of his suits left over from his banking days. He knew his ties were no longer in fashion, but one would be fine for a country funeral.

He had barely stopped when he saw the front door open. Sedalia came out in a plain black dress with her hair down instead of tied back. Her dark brunette hair was shoulder length and glistened in the sunlight. She looked stunning. He tried not to stare, but he knew she could tell he was looking.

When she got in he said, "My, don't you look glamorous."

"You look rather handsome yourself. I don't think I've seen you wearing a tie before."

"It's not among my favorite things to wear." Clay added, "I once heard that over on Tangier Island in the Chesapeake Bay if a boy wanted to compliment a girl, instead of saying she was good looking, he'd say, 'You ain't ugly none.'" Looking quizzical, Sedalia answered, "If that was a compliment, thanks."

As they drove, Clay felt something in his inside coat pocket. He pulled it out and it was a handout from the last funeral he attended. One of the problems with getting older was the increasing number of funerals. He had been to Catholic, Baptist, Methodist, Episcopal, Jewish and both black and white funerals. Some had hymns or songs sung to guitar or piano accompaniment. Others had clapping in unison along with the choir's singing. Most had lunch served afterwards. They were all a little different.

When they arrived at the church the parking lot was already full and people were parking on both sides of the country road. Two county sheriff deputies were slowing down and directing traffic and later would lead and direct the traffic for the funeral procession to the graveyard. He and Sedalia walked into the church and searched for a seat. He saw familiar faces—Robert, Corine and Ant Mabel. Most looked stoic and somber, but smiled with eye contact. Ant Mabel winked. Burl caught Clay's eye and he looked down the pew and got people to move closer together to make more room for him and Sedalia. Burl leaned over and whispered, "Someone's going to pay for this; you just wait and see." Clay nodded in agreement. It seemed people were staring at Sedalia. No one, himself included, had ever seen her so dressed up.

It was still about twenty minutes before one o'clock. Mack's friendly face and good humor would be missed by everyone. Clay glanced around and saw Cecil and his wife, Woodrow and his wife, Bull, Bill Ware and Walter Stringfellow. Everyone was dressed to the hilt. Most of the men had on coats and ties, and the women were well dressed and quite a few wore hats. Chairs were brought in and set along the walls, the back, and both sides of the center aisle. Some men were standing along the back wall and in the vestibule.

Around ten minutes to one the choir stood up and began singing a subdued, but uplifting spiritual. Clay knew Sedalia had never been to a black funeral and wondered what she was thinking. She reached over and squeezed his hand.

After the choir sat down, the front side door opened and Lula came in, supported on each side by her two sons. Her head was bowed and she was crying. She held a handkerchief to her face. Tears were also streaming down her sons' faces and you could see their anguish. They were followed by the rest of her family, their spouses, aunts, uncles, grandchildren and cousins. A couple of the grandchildren were taking it hard. Mack loved his grandchildren and they would certainly miss him.

The church's pastor, Reverend Lewis, stood up and was visibly emotional. The closed casket sat on a stand in front of the pulpit. Reverend Lewis took off his glasses and cleaned them and took a drink of water. He started to speak but nothing came out. He stepped back, took his handkerchief again and wiped his forehead and started to speak again. He only got out a few words before he again stepped back and cleared his throat. Then he started talking about Mack with tears rolling down his cheeks. He told how Mack had spent so much of his life helping the church and others in the community. He slowly hit his stride and with voice rising said, "This is not an occasion to get all teary eyed and sad. This is a celebration of the life of Mack Brown." He went on praising Mack and all the good deeds he had done. Clay felt a lump in his throat and tears welling up, and he saw Sedalia dabbing with a tissue.

After Reverend Lewis finished, a lady stood up and sang without accompaniment a beautiful rendition of "Precious Lord Take My Hand." It was moving and as well done as any he had ever heard on tape, CD, or TV. She was followed by preachers of other black churches who talked about their memories of Mack. They said things like, "If Mack said he was going to do something you could count on it being done," and, "If you asked Mack his opinion he would tell you in a nice way what he thought and not something he thought you might want to hear," and, "He loved to joke and tease and have fun. There won't many times he won't laughing or smiling," and, "He said don't worry about your wants, worry about your needs."

Willie Massie got up and talked about the activities of the hunt club and trips the fishing club took on the Chesapeake Bay. Clay didn't know there was a black hunt or fishing club, but he knew Mack liked to hunt and fish and most of the stories Willie told were about funny experiences that had happened where Mack was the victim or the instigator. Sounds of subdued laughs were mingled with sniffles.

When Clay glanced at his watch it was almost three o'clock and the service was not over. Then a woman preacher got up and said a life, death, and going to heaven prayer that was so powerfully delivered it sounded like a sermon. Clay opened his eyes to watch her and noticed others had lifted their heads and were doing the same.

The final hymn began slowly. The song seemed to be about what heaven was going to be like. The piano player began to increase the tempo. The chorus was something like, "No more Mondays, Tuesdays, Wednesdays, no more Thursdays, Fridays, Saturdays when I'm with the Lord." Gradually the congregation started standing up until everyone in the church was singing loudly and clapping and swaying. Clay felt more religious than he had in a long time.

When all the music and accolades finally ended it was almost four o'clock. Where had the time gone? Clay looked at Sedalia; she was smiling through tear tracks. Afterwards, people milled around talking. Robert's mother, Ant Mabel, came over and spoke to Clay. "When you comin' back to visit me? You said 'lass' year you'd be back in a week or two. You ought to be 'shamed of yoself, and who's this pretty thing with you? Don't tell me you been courtin' and not told me. I don't know what I'm goin' to do with you."

Clay felt his face flush.

"Ant Mabel, you are so bad, and I believe you're gettin' worse with age. This is my good neighbor, Sedalia."

"I know. Robert told me 'bout how much she helped out when Troop got burned and how people take animals to her that get hurt. Miss Sedalia, it's a pleasure to finally meet you. Robert also said somethin' 'bout how smart you are and how you seemed to know some things before they happen."

Now Sedalia blushed. "Ant Mabel, you know better than anyone how Robert likes to tell tall tales."

"You right 'bout that, girl, and if this boy here ever says anything bad 'bout me, you jus' let me know and I'll tell you three times as many 'bout him."

They all smiled and Ant Mabel added, "Why don't you bring this sweet lady to see me? She might have something sensible to say instead of all that foolishness you go on about." Ant Mabel laughed and said, "Gotta go. See Robert lookin' at me; we goin' to the cemetery. Now, you bring her with you, you hear?"

When they got in the Jeep, Sedalia said, "That's the most moving funeral I've ever been to. Somehow I feel happy, sad, and peaceful all at the same time. I think I might start back to church again if I could find one like this."

On the way home Clay asked if she would like to ride with him to Lynchburg tomorrow to see Troop and she said yes, so he told her he'd pick her up around ten o'clock. He also asked if she'd like to go visit Ant Mabel sometime and she said, "Yeah, that might be fun."

CHAPTER 10

Saying:
If brains were taxable, he'd be due a refund.

After dropping Sedalia off at her house, Clay decided to go by Rucker's for some milk and bread, cereal, and sliced meat and cheese for sandwiches. Cecil's deli menu had been growing so he got fried chicken to go for dinner. Woodcutters, farm workers, highway department employees, tradesmen, and locals came in to grab some lunch and dinner. Some got it to go, others stood around the counter or sat at a couple of tables and ate and talked.

Clay got his groceries and wandered over to where Burl and the hard core locals and old timers sat. Burl had come straight from church, had taken off his tie and unbuttoned the top two buttons around his ample neck. He was going on about some robbery yesterday at the Piedmont National Branch in Bedford.

"They say the guy wearing a ski mask came in right at closing time, won't but a couple of customers in the bank. He pulled out his pistol and yelled for everybody to hit the floor and told the employees not to be pushin' no buttons. They say he told Buddy Ebbers, the branch manager, that meant him, too, said he called Buddy a low-life, pencil-neck, four-eyed, bugle nose son of a bitch and told him if he made a false move he'd just as soon blow his head off as look at 'em. He told the tellers to put their 10s and 20s in the bag he passed down the line and not to put any of that 'funny money' in the bag."

Bull piped up, "Sounds like he might of known ole Buddy personally."

Everyone laughed and Burl continued, "Said on the news he got away with around $6000. Said he ran in the woods behind the bank. They think he had a 4x4 vehicle hidden out of sight."

Clay spoke up, "Reminds me of the time we had an FBI agent talk to our tellers about what to do in a robbery. He told about a robber that held up a bank and a teller gave him the exploding dye package of twenties they used to keep. He stuffed all the money in his pockets and ran out of the bank. About halfway across the parking lot the package exploded in his back pocket. Said the guy was hoppin' around, screaming, and fanning his butt. On top of that he was covered with purple dye. Don't think they use the exploding dye anymore—tellers could accidentally hurt themselves, but they do keep 'bait money' to give the robbers. The bank keeps a list of serial numbers so if it shows up in circulation it might give a lead as to who stole it."

Cecil wandered by the group and mentioned to Clay to come aside and he told him Ole Rip's brother, Easel, was in here again this afternoon. "He stood around awhile and then left—he's up to something—it's a real puzzle. I get the impression he's snoopin', but everyone had gone to the funeral so he left, didn't buy anything, never said nothing. I did notice that rank odor again after he left."

Burl, overhearing Ole Devil Rip's name, piped up, "You reckon Ole Rip is still farmin' in the woods?" Everyone knew he meant making moonshine whiskey.

Bull chimed in, "I hear he's been makin' it for years. The revenue agents just can't catch him at it or find his still."

Bill Ware followed, "Old timers said there was a big cave in that mountain; said Ole Rip's barn backs right up to the opening; said there was a hidden door at the back of the barn that opened into the cave."

Woodrow added, "I've heard he only cooks at night, you know that's why they call it moonshine, so nobody ever sees the smoke. If he makes it in the cave they probably have another opening to vent the smoke and the smell. Course, these days they say moonshiners cook with propane. They say that cave goes way back under that mountain."

Clay recalled, "Seems like I remember when I was growing up that Piney River between Amherst and Nelson counties used to be the moonshine center for these parts. I also remember that movie *Thunder Road* with Robert Mitchum. Some of the men who drove the cars that hauled moonshine turned out to be some of NASCAR's best early drivers, and they knew all kinds of tricks like being able to swap ends at full speed and go in the opposite direction. Sometimes they'd send a fast driver with no whiskey as a decoy so the revenuers would chase him, and the one carrying it would drive at normal speed and not be noticed. One driver used to make a run on Sunday afternoon with his wife and family all dressed up like they'd just come from church."

Burl then said, "Transporting it was one thing, but making it was another, and where they put the still got real creative. It was probably a lie, but I heard one of those snake handling preachers over in West Virginia had a still in the basement of a church in a room behind where he kept all those copperheads and rattlesnakes. Won't no agent going to walk through a roomful of rattlesnakes. I do know they found a still underground of what looked like a graveyard, with fake headstones on a grassy lawn over the top."

Thinking of what Cecil had said, Clay motioned him to come away from the group and asked, "What do you really think about Ole Rip's brother coming in here? It makes me wonder if it might somehow be connected to Troop getting beat up. What's your take on all this?"

"It's hard to say, but I've got my suspicions. Ole Rip won't too bad when he was younger—just a tall, strong, hard workin' man. One time he came upon a wreck over on Mossy Rock Road. One of the Burgess boys had fallen out the front door and the car rolled on him. Ole Rip was one of the first to come up the road. They say he lifted the whole rear end off that boy while someone pulled him out. Anyway, he had a good wife, Annie, everything he won't—a friendly, cheerful church-going woman. Anyway, Annie got some kind of cancer and went down fast. After that it looked like Ole Rip didn't care anymore and really went bad. He still cuts some timber, but most people round here won't deal with him 'cause they know he'll short 'em. They have two boys and the rumor is that the reason they always have fancy new, big, pickups is money from moonshine."

Clay was incredulous, "After all these years you'd think they would have caught him."

Cecil responded, "The revenuers raided him several years ago, but they didn't find anything. It was said they spent more time fightin' off that pack of dogs than they did lookin' for the stuff. His place is up a long hollow and he keeps a lookout with a walkie-talkie or probably a cell phone now. He knows they're coming twenty minutes before they get there—plenty of time to camouflage the cave entrance if that's where the still is. His lookouts also go round the rest of the land in case anyone tries to sneak in from the backside. His brother Easel is one of the lookouts and he's meaner than Rip. Wouldn't surprise me none if he might know something about what happened to Troop. Might be why he's snoopin' 'round over here; anyhow, Ole Rip owns over 1000 acres in those mountains and he deliberately keeps the road rough so no regular car can travel it."

Cecil continued, "He don't seem to care how much trouble those boys get into. They've been locked up I don't know how many times for fist fights in bars, drivin' drunk, racing and reckless drivin'. Sometimes the police chase 'em and they get away by going up some wood road they know the cops can't follow. They know every wood road and back road in Somerset County. If they shot the whole bunch it wouldn't be no big loss. Luckily, they have stayed on the other side of the mountain in the past, but recently his boys have become friends with Earl's boy, Junior. Earl is the one who has the trucking business. Junior's mother, Betty Lou, has spoiled him rotten. All he does is build and race hot rods. Earl built him a complete shop with all the tools you can name to rebuild engines and make repairs, plus a hydraulic lift, drill press, lathe, everything. Earl makes out that Junior keeps his tractors running, but I know Junior don't know nothin' about diesels. And, Betty Lou, you've seen her riding around in that powder blue restored '68 Cadillac Deville convertible with her hair up in a beehive hair-do and mascara as heavy as Tammy Faye Baker used to wear. She's always chewing gum with her mouth open and has an irritated, arrogant expression as if you are below her class. I don't know how Earl makes enough money for Junior's hot rods and Betty Lou's spending habits. They both stay on Earl's case all the time; and he still has enough money to buy rental property. He owns seven or eight rental houses. It just don't add up. Trucking ain't as lucrative as it used to be, what with competition, cost of rigs and diesel fuel. Maybe that western run for the furniture company is bigger than we thought. He's got an agent that spends a lot of time on the phone looking for back hauls so his drivers won't have to dead head back empty. He's got another deal hauling lumber down to Florida, and another one hauling apple products down Texas way. On top of that, he owns an oceanfront house in either Duck or Kitty Hawk. Betty Lou likes to spend most of May and September down there. Earl drives a Lexus. Burl said it looked like an upscale Camry to him. Anyway, Earl don't strike me as being all that smart, but you can't tell how smart someone is by how they look or talk." Cecil spotted a customer waiting and said, "Got to get to work, tell you more later."

It was getting dark and it had been a long day, so Clay headed home.

CHAPTER 11

Saying:
He who laughs last thinks slowest.

Clay picked up Sedalia promptly at ten o'clock. She was dressed in her more typical attire—white sweatshirt, weathered leather jacket and faded jeans. She smelled like fresh sun-dried laundry and there was a hint of something else that smelled good. She took off her jacket and put it on the seat between them.

She began, "Before I forget, I've got to tell you about a dream I had last night. It was more like a nightmare. There was a tall, sinister man sneaking up in the dark behind a man who was sitting on a log in front of a small fire. He had a long, thick walking stick and he was gripping it with both hands like a baseball player ready to swing. I knew he was going to hit the man, but I must have been making noises because the dogs woke me up nuzzling me and whining; it was very disturbing. I couldn't get back to sleep."

"That's definitely a weird dream. What do you think it means?"

"I don't know, but it was too real."

"It reminds me of the character I saw at Rucker's the day before Mack's funeral. Cecil said he was Ole Rip's brother and he wondered why he was hanging around. Both Burl and Cecil say Ole Rip's clan is a mean bunch. You've probably seen his two boys hot-roddin' in those big black pickups; they mostly stay on the other side of the mountain, except when they come over to get with Earl Dooley's son, Junior. There's often trouble when they get together. The sheriff's office knows them well."

Sedalia asked, "Wonder if they might have had anything to do with Mack's wreck? They could have been drag racing and Mack lost control trying to avoid them."

"It's what a few of us suspect."

"I worry that someone else will die before this is over. I've got a bad feeling about it. I fear things will get a lot more violent than our experience with T. Wayne."

By now they were through Somerset and well on the way to Lynchburg.

Sedalia continued, "We've got to look out for Troop's animals till we find out if he's going to be okay."

Clay added, "Another thing is we'll have to look after him until he can make it on his own again. He can stay with me while he's on the mend. Troop would be good company, but any kind of confinement will be hard on him. I've never heard of him being married or talking about any family so there's probably no one to come and stay with him. I've heard he might have some distant kin among the Monacan Indians in Amherst County. I'll check at their Mission to see if anyone knows."

Clay asked at the information desk for Troop's room number and condition. The attendant said he was still in intensive care and there was no change.

When they went to see him, an older nurse was coming out of the intensive care unit. She said he was stable and doing as well as could be expected. She said she thought she'd seen a finger move, but it was probably just a muscle twitch.

He was hooked up to all kinds of hanging bottles with tubes and IVs and his head was wrapped up in bandages. His face was swollen and there were stitches beside his eye. It was hard for Clay to look at Troop on life support as he remembered how lean and healthy he had always been. Sedalia took Troop's hand and held it in both of hers and spoke softly. She hoped that at least subconsciously he could hear her.

Clay excused himself to go to the bathroom. When he came back the nurse was talking with Sedalia. She looked serious and had a no-nonsense attitude.

"He's my project, and I'm not going to give up on 'em. I try not to get too attached, but I'm getting kinda close to this ole fellow. The other nurses feel the same way. He's tough as nails. He might come around when this swelling goes down. Early on the doctors talked about removing a part of his skull to let his swollen brain expand, but decided not to. They did a CT scan and an MRI and found there were no skull fractures."

CHAPTER 12

Church Bulletin:
Weight Watchers will meet at 7 p.m. at First Presbyterian Church.
Please use the large double door at the side entrance.

Before leaving town, Clay got an idea and asked Sedalia if she had ever eaten at the Texas Inn. She said she'd never heard of it.

"Are you game to try something different?"

"I guess so." She looked apprehensive.

Clay turned into the Texas Inn, better known as the "Tea Room," but all the spaces in front were taken so he parked in the adjoining lot.

He explained that the Tea Room was originally a Pure Oil gas station, white with a blue roof, converted years ago to a limited menu diner type restaurant. "You might see someone in a business suit, but most of the clientele are workers and tradesmen grabbing a quick lunch. The Texas Inn specialties are chili, hot dogs and cheesy westerns. A cheesy western is a hamburger, a slice of cheese and a fried egg and their special recipe of relish, and you don't add lettuce or tomato to it. There are about fifteen stools around an "L" shaped counter with three women waitresses, two grill cooks and someone cooking in the back. The waitresses, well, I'll let you see and hear for yourself." When they entered, Clay spotted two stools together so he grabbed them.

The waitress smiled and asked, "Whatcha want, honey?" She called everyone honey, even the women.

Clay said, "Hot all the way, bowl and a Dr. Pepper."

She yelled, "Hot all the way and a bowl."

The other waitresses were doing the same thing—how the cook kept all those orders in his head is hard to imagine. Clay said, "The waitresses sometimes get in arguments and heated discussions with each other, the cooks and the customers. The night crew is even wilder, especially when some of the rowdy party types come in late. The Tea Room is open 24/6. They close on Sunday." Sedalia looked at the menu sign on the wall; thoroughly confused, she said she'd have the same and a diet Coke. She asked Clay what a "funny" was. He told her it was a hot dog bun with all the fixings but no weiner.

"Y'all want glasses?" Clay nodded affirmatively. Service was almost instant. Sedalia tentatively tasted her choices and said the chili was different but good, and the hot dog with chili, relish and onions was delicious. It didn't take long to eat and they were soon on their way home.

"Well, what do you think?"

"It's definitely different, it was kinda crazy, but I liked it, no writing orders or getting a check, just yell it out. Let's do it again the next time we come over."

Sedalia changed the subject to Troop. "He's in there—he's got a bright white aura. I felt something when I was holding his hand, like energy. Even if he comes around though, there may be memory loss or brain damage; we've got to find out who did this. It's not likely the law will find who did it; there are no obvious clues and he had no enemies."

They stopped off at Rucker's to pick up some dog food and Sedalia and Clay needed a few groceries. Only Burl and Bill Ware were there keeping the seats warm. Burl raised an eyebrow at Clay when he saw Sedalia, but he only spoke and asked about Troop. They filled them in and asked if there was any news. There was none so Clay got his groceries, some dry and canned dog food and 25 pounds of scratch feed for the chickens.

Before going to Troop's house they stopped to check on Blue. Blue was hobbling around on three legs and growled at Clay, then wagged his tail when Sedalia reached to pet him. Dew and Gladys came out on the porch. Clay told Gladys, "He sure looks a lot better," and then added, "I don't know why that dog doesn't like me."

After leaving some of the dog food for Blue, they drove to Troop's cabin. Before getting out of the truck, Sedalia asked, "Have you talked with Robert about Mack?"

"Yeah, we talked a long time last night. He and Mack were real close. They hunted and fished together and went to the same church. Robert sometimes holds things in, but I know he's torn up."

"What does he think happened?"

"He believes Mack was trying to avoid something. Robert knows about Rip's boys and Junior. He's seen them drag racing before on that section of road. Mack was coming down the hill before the bridge and the long, straight stretch. If they were going flat out or playing "chicken" he believes Mack swerved to avoid a head-on and lost it. As you know, Robert knows a lot from being an investigator in the CID in the army. I've got a feeling he's going to look a little deeper into things. I wouldn't want Robert for an enemy."

Walking up to Troop's, Clay marveled at how well he had laid out the cabin, the barn, the chicken house, the woodshed, and the garden. The small but bold creek wound down beside the garden. Water from a clean mountain spring above the cabin flowed through the springhouse where he stored milk and butter in buckets in a trough. Like a refrigerator, the cold spring water kept the contents fresh and cool. Everything fitted together in harmony and common sense.

Sedalia opened a can of dog food and split it between Ruby and Buckshot. They "woofed" it down in hound-like fashion, Clay filled a pan on the porch with the dry dog food. He opened the bag

51

of scratch feed for the chickens and poured some in the feeder and scattered some on the bare ground. Sedalia went in the chicken house and gathered up the brown shell eggs.

"You think we ought to give Millie and Mabeline some hay?" she asked.

"Wouldn't hurt and I still haven't found out about the bees. You're going to laugh but Walter did say something odd about bees. Walter doesn't joke around, and he said it straight face serious. He said, and I won't stammer for effect, 'You've got to tell the bees about Troop, if you don't they'll swarm and leave.' He said bees recognize their keeper and if they don't see him or her for a long while they will leave."

"You're kidding."

"That's what he said. I don't think they'd do it, especially in cold weather, but it can't hurt. You want to tell 'em, or me?"

Sedalia looked at Clay as if he were pulling her leg.

"I can see you don't believe me, so I guess I'll have to do it, but you've got to promise you won't tell anyone."

Laughing, she promised.

Clay walked close to the beehive and noticed some dead bees around the entrance. He knew the workers kicked out the drones in cold weather because they would consume part of the winter food supply; the workers knew how to make new drones in the spring. Glancing back and feeling foolish, he spoke softly to the bees and explained that Troop was sick, but he would be coming home soon.

Sedalia was grinning from ear to ear when he walked back.

"What did you say?"

"I told them the grinning woman was crazy."

She laughed, and asked, "Didn't you say Millie is supposed to have a calf soon?"

"Yeah, I remember Troop bringing her down to breed her to my bull. She ought to be calving in a month or two."

"How'd he get her down to your place?"

"He put a halter on her head and led her down the road. He didn't really need a halter—Millie would have followed him anywhere, but he used a halter in case a vehicle might come by and frighten her." Clay added, "Guess we're through here. We've got our own animals to look after. You ready to go?"

"Yeah, it's been a full day, but a good one."

Clay let Sedalia out among her menagerie and said, "Bye, keep in touch."

"You do the same; let me know if you hear anything." She held his glance a moment longer than usual.

CHAPTER 13

Epitaph for a Waiter: "At last God caught his eye."
—Harry Secombe

After driving the short distance to his house, Clay got his mail from the mailbox and was greeted by Jake and Rita when he got out of his truck. The November sun had now gone behind the mountains—it got dark earlier when daylight savings time changed. The temperature was dropping and shadows covered the valley below. The cattle were still lying where the last sunshine had been. Cattle find the best places to bed down when the weather is cold. His father said to always feed 'em where you find 'em—they know the best place to be, but Clay knew to move the hay around to spread the manure in the pasture.

Clay plopped in his recliner, turned the TV on to the local news channel, put it on closed caption and hit the mute button and shuffled through the mail. His trash can was beside his chair, and sometimes he wondered how many trees were needed every day for junk and advertising mail.

A nap was tempting, but a nap this late made it hard to sleep later so he got out his guitar. After checking the strings on his tuner he started strumming some of his favorites "Me and Bobby McGhee," "Wabash Canon Ball," "House of the Rising Sun," and "Country Roads." He could play and sing as loudly as he liked, knowing no one would hear. Afterwards he flipped through his pile of songs and pulled out "Folsom Prison Blues." They say Merle Haggard was sitting on the front row when Johnny Cash sang at the Folsom Prison Concert.

He felt energized afterwards as he thawed and heated the frozen stuffed peppers, fixed two pieces of whole wheat toast dusted with parmesan cheese and opened a cup of applesauce.

After dinner he watched the evening news and thought about the day's events. Jake pushed his muzzle in his lap to be petted, and then collapsed beside his chair and went to sleep. Nothing of interest was on TV so he went to the bookcase and rummaged through his old favorites. Rereading favorite books was becoming a frequent pastime. He pulled out Harper Lee's *To Kill a Mockingbird* and started reading.

Soon, though, his mind flitted back to the group's experience with Sally's murder. He recalled finding the knife and finding the threatening note in his mailbox. The note said to put what they found in the old mailbox at the deserted Wheeler place by 12 o'clock Saturday night or else.

The knife the group had found appeared to have come from an upscale set that had the brand name and model number. He got the idea of getting a duplicate knife and scuffing it up to look used and put it in the mailbox. He drove to Barracks Road Shopping Center in Charlottesville for advice. The store specialized in fancy cutlery and cookware. They carried the line and he bought an exact match.

On Saturday night, not knowing what to expect, Robert and Troop staked out the mailbox while he and Sedalia sat outside on the front porch and watched and listened. A little after twelve, Robert and Troop came back to the house and said a young man had picked up the knife. They joined Clay and Sedalia and as the night wore on they began to think the switch had worked. Then they heard it! It was a loud explosion from a high powered rifle, and simultaneously a high-pitched scream from Blackjack. They rushed down to see Blackjack thrashing back and forth trying to get up, but when he was shot he had reared up and came down off balance and broke his front leg. The memory of holding Blackjack's head in his arms was too painful—the fear in his eyes was heartbreaking. Clay talked and tried to comfort his spirited companion, but he knew he had to be put down. Robert volunteered to shoot him. He, Sedalia, and Troop were walking back to the house when Robert put the 38 behind Blackjack's ear and pulled the trigger. They turned to see Blackjack quivering and then go limp. Pepper, his other horse, went up to Blackjack and tried to nuzzle him to get up. When she realized something was terribly wrong, she gave a long, high-pitched whinny.

No sooner had they gotten to the house than the phone rang. The shooter said, "You think we can't tell old from new. You put the knife in the mailbox by twelve tonight or else." The shooter then threatened to kill all four if he didn't. The group believed that shooting Black Jack was to let them know they meant business.

That's when the team went to work. Because the shooter had killed Blackjack they were able to get media coverage and state police support. That night Robert and a state police swat team set up night cameras and caught the pickup man who turned out to be a kid who had been paid to do the pickup. The real excitement came when Troop caught the shooter's leg in a trap he had set on the backside of Clay's farm. Two other police swat team members had been strategically staked out along the road below the house on Little Spruce Road. Troop had wisely figured it would be easier for a hit man to sneak in over the ridge and through the woods, so he had set a couple of snare traps in an old roadbed by bending strong saplings and tying them to a circular rope staked on the ground. A trigger released the trap if anything, or anyone, stepped in the circle. When the shooter stepped in and sprung the trap it caught his leg. When Troop arrived, the shooter was trying to keep his balance by frantically hopping around on his other leg and taking wild shots at Blue. Blue had him by the pants leg and was jerking and growling and keeping him off balance. Troop yelled at the man, "You shoot my dog, you're gonna die." The shooter looked at Troop and yelled, "Drop your gun ole man—you ain't got a chance." Seeing Troop had only a single barrel shotgun, he said, "Hell, you only got one shot."

Troop answered, "Double-aught buckshot—don't need but one shot."

The shooter then saw a red dot bouncing around on his chest and threw down his gun. A swat team officer had heard the shots and rushed to the scene.

They escorted the shooter back to the house and no sooner had they all assembled than Clay collapsed. Sedalia yelled, "He's having a heart attack!" Even though the police knew CPR, Sedalia took over. He had stopped breathing and she couldn't get a pulse. She did mouth-to-mouth resuscitation and compressions, and after five tries she felt a pulse and after what seemed forever, she got him breathing. The hit man claimed his contract was done over the phone and he didn't know who paid it.

CHAPTER 14

Never get in a fight with an ugly person—
they have nothing to lose.
—Anonymous

Wednesday morning Corine and Robert stopped by Rucker's to pick up some groceries. Robert had an arm leaning against a gondola, watching Corine shop. She was an aisle away putting stuff in a hand basket when he got a side view of Earl's son, Junior, and another guy walking by. Corine, a strikingly handsome and shapely woman, was bent over getting something from the bottom shelf. Junior hesitated and stared at her butt and exclaimed in a leering tone, "All right!" Robert heard him and hellfire and rage flew into him. He yelled at Junior, "What did you say?"

Junior at 6'2" and 220 lbs had played linebacker in high school. He turned and glared at Robert and said, "What's it to you?"

"I heard what you said and you don't talk about my wife like that."

"I'll talk anyway I damn well please!"

"Maybe you'd like to take it outside and learn some manners."

Junior, like most bullies, was basically a coward. He sized up Robert and knew he was outmanned. His demeanor did a complete reversal and he said, "Sorry man, I didn't know she was your wife. I didn't mean no disrespect."

There was a moment like freezing a timeframe, Robert decided to let it slide and finally said, "No problem." Junior and his friend walked away. Robert saw them whispering, and Junior's friend glared back.

"What was that all about?" asked Corine.

Robert was regaining his composure. "He made some remark about your nice butt."

Corine half grinned and said, "You gotta watch yo mouth—it's getting so I can't take you anywhere."

CHAPTER 15

Lead me not into temptation—I can find it myself.

Fall had slowly turned to winter. During the night Clay heard the heavy rain falling on the tin roof. Sometimes he slept through storms, but this rain was loud and incessant. It was still coming down at daybreak. Looking out the back door toward the barn he saw large puddles and a heavy runoff was flowing down the ditches beside the road. He stirred the coals in the wood stove and added some dry wood to get it started. After grinding the coffee and adding water, he sat down, petted Jake and Rita, and waited for the coffeemaker to make its gurgling sound. Sometimes rainy days were cozy and comfortable; others were gloomy or depressing. It was also lonely as he realized how much he missed his wife. He watched the cardinals, blue jays and sparrows at the feeder. They seemed energetic as if the rain were invigorating. Steam was rising off the cows that were milling around a large round of hay. They didn't seem to mind the discomfort of being wet and cold. He drank the coffee and sat in a quiet reflective mood.

Even though it was cold, it was warmer than the previous day, which created a heavy fog. Pepper, his Appaloosa mare, came around to the barn. Ever since Blackjack was killed, she seemed to crave affection. Maybe he would go to the horse sale in Lexington and buy another horse. He went to the barn, followed by Jake, to check the calves. Pepper came running and stuck her head over the fence. The air was crisp and it always smelled better in the rain. It seemed to accentuate the scents of hay, cows, and manure. In the summer the smell of the electronically charged air after a thunderstorm gave the air a purified fragrance. He thought about the intoxicating smells of just-cut grass or hay, honeysuckle and fresh cut watermelon.

Clay's mind was focused on the incident Robert told him he had with Junior. It was people like Junior you had to watch. He was like a dog that looked shy and harmless, but would sneak around and bite you from behind. Junior was like someone who smiled to your face, and then did something sneaky behind your back.

Junior and Ole Rip's boys, Axle and Rance, were bad news. They seemed to think they were bulletproof. Clay couldn't help believing they had something to do with Mack's death. How would anyone ever know? Maybe Sedalia and Robert would have some ideas. It seemed like a flashback to when the sheriff arrested Dew for the murder of Sally. How many bad things happen where the culprit is never found or a murder gets classified as an accident?

Through the kitchen window he could see the fog rolling slowly, allowing occasional dim views of the trees and the blurred outline of the hilltop behind the barn. He knew he had to get up and do something. There were always things to do on a farm—repairs, bookwork, cleaning, sharpening, lubricating, etc., but a rainy morning was a good time to go to Rucker's. He knew Burl, Woodrow, Bill Ware and others would likely be there. Bull probably wouldn't be hauling stone today and Robert might come by. The decision was easy.

He was right; the rain had brought them all in, including Professor Willis, the Sweet Briar professor. The group was animated and Professor Willis was saying, "I think more people go to church for social reasons than religion. I bet if preachers asked people to write a paragraph about the sermon afterwards, half of them couldn't write a sentence."

Woodrow followed, "You got that right. Some of those pious sisters just want to see what the other women are wearing and take notes on who is absent."

"And what about these televangelists," exclaimed Bill. "Hank Williams, Jr. has a song with a verse that says they want you to send your money to the Lord, but they give you their address."

The group laughed, and Robert chimed in, "Just deliver me from those born again Christians trying to save my soul. The reason some of 'em got saved was they couldn't stand their guilt from all the bad things they'd done."

Woodrow followed, musing, "How much fun can you really have before you go to hell?"

Burl came back with, "And I've heard there's a good Baptist hiding inside every alcoholic. 'Course, if you're an Episcopalian, you don't have to feel guilty about drinking."

Burl continued, "This talk about religion reminds me of the time that squirrel got in the tent revival they were having in the field beside the old Evergreen school. That squirrel was so terrified and disoriented he ran up the first thing he saw, which just happened to be old lady Givens' leg. Talk about pandemonium! They said Gerty was pulling her dress up way above modesty, hopping around and cussing saying 'goddamn' every other word. I wish I'd been there."

Clay added, "Did anyone think about the poor squirrel? After what he saw he won't ever be the same—bet he kept his distance from humans from then on."

Everyone was laughing and Professor Willis said, "Religion used to be more interesting. Remember when we had Oral Roberts, Jim and Tammy Faye Baker and Jimmy Swaggart? I miss all that crying and pleading and mascara."

"How do you feel about Jerry Falwell, rest his soul, and Pat Robertson?" asked Woodrow.

"As you know, being a college professor, I live in a somewhat closed environment. I have to get out with crazy people like you to find out what real people think. I know a psychiatrist who goes to a biker bar to get away from his patients. Anyway, in Jerry's case I think he did a lot of good things, like starting Liberty University and Thomas Road Baptist Church, establishing a home for unwed mothers, and an alcoholic rehab place. He never lived extravagantly and his wife jerked his chain when he got out of line, like with the Teletubbies. His two sons seem to be doing well. In Jerry's case, both Reverend Sharpton and Larry Flint said they disagreed with him on almost everything, but liked him personally. Pat Robertson seems to be a good man. He, Reverend Sharpton and Jessie Jackson would all be better off if they stayed out of politics. By the way, they say Jerry's father hauled some moonshine, but his mother was a rock solid Christian. His dad was also a very successful businessman. I heard the moonshine was for his restaurant customers."

"Speaking about Reverend Sharpton and Reverend Jackson, how do you feel about them?" asked Robert.

There was a hush.

The professor gave a nervous laugh.

"I wish you hadn't asked me that."

"Why?"

"I don't know how you feel about them, and I consider you a friend and I don't want to hurt your feelings."

Robert grinned, "Go ahead, I can handle it, and I probably won't hold it against you."

"Okay, but the only thing I'm going to say is I think they are both more interested in staying in the limelight of controversy than doing God's work. The media, of course, is partly to blame because they thrive on dissention and controversy. By the way, they both condemned the Duke Lacrosse team before they were given a hearing. The DA was later censored by The North Carolina Bar Association, but things went on at that party that were way out of line. The black dancers were no angels either. One was on parole, and the other was later charged with killing her boyfriend."

"I guess that's a fair answer. I mostly agree."

Clay gave a sigh of relief and added, "What scares the hell out of me, no pun intended, are zealots and radical preachers that get people to follow them and end up in tragedies like Jonestown and Waco. Along the same line, extremist politicians, both Republicans and Democrats, are just as scary."

CHAPTER 16

Atheist's Funeral—All dressed up and nowhere to go.

The time had flown, but it was just 11 o'clock so Clay decided to drive to Lynchburg and check on Troop. The sky was overcast, but the rain had stopped. Troop was still in intensive care, but his guardian angel nurse seemed less tense—she actually smiled.

"Saw a good sign this morning. He moved his left arm and fingers. I pinched his thumb and I know he felt it. I've seen his eyelids flutter, and at times he's restless. Even though the side rails are up, we keep him restrained with these cloth wrist and leg restraints so he won't accidentally pull out the IVs or pull off the bandages."

"That's the best news yet."

"I think the swelling is going down, but he's got a long way to go, and nobody knows if his mind and memory will be affected." She patted Troop's hand and left the room. Clay sat a few minutes and then took Troop's hand and spoke, "It's me, Troop. Clay. In case you can hear me, we are all pulling for you—Robert, Sedalia and all the gang at Rucker's. Hang in there partner. All your animals are fine. Sedalia and I are checking on them every day."

On the way back he stopped at the Silver Pig in Madison Heights and got a delicious BBQ sandwich with slaw and extra hot sauce and a cup of water. He stopped at Wal-Mart and ate in the parking lot while listening to one of his old tapes by Kinky Friedman and the Texas Jewboys. Some of the songs were sung by Kinky, but most were sung by his friends Willie, Delbert, Dwight Yoakum, Marty Stuart, Lyle Lovett, and others. Kinky is a funny, sarcastic, schizophrenic Jewish cowboy from Texas who believes the lone star of Texas is the Star of David. He was the first full-blooded

Jew to appear on the Grand Ole Opry. His funniest song, "They Ain't Makin' Jews Like Jesus Anymore," manages to insult blacks, whites, and Jews. His songs will make you laugh or cry or, in one case, sick ("Ole Ben Lucas Had a Lot of Mucus"). He ran for governor of Texas in 2006 and received 13 percent of the vote. One of the things he was in favor of was gay marriage. He said gays had every right to be as miserable as the rest of us. He also wanted to change the Ten Commandments to the ten suggestions.

Riding home, his mind flashed back to his heart attack after Black Jack was shot. He woke up in the hospital surrounded by Robert, Troop and Sedalia. They told him he had had a mild heart attack and that rest, exercise, and a lean, healthy diet would soon put him back in good shape. A few days later he was being wheeled from his room to go home. Sedalia rolled him slowly by the sheriff's room. The turmoil and stress of the state police entering Sally's murder investigation had caused the sheriff to have a massive stroke. He was slumped in a wheelchair and his wife was dabbing his drool. He glanced at Clay, grunted and gave a slight lurch forward. Sedalia told him the sheriff was paralyzed on his right side and couldn't speak. A little later they learned that T. Wayne was missing and wanted for questioning about Sally's murder.

The memories were flowing back. Clay was steadily recovering from his heart attack. He was anxious to get out and persuaded Sedalia to go with him for a day trip to Charlottesville. He delighted in showing her where to turn to go to Schuyler where Earl Hamner, who wrote *Spencer's Mountain* (The Waltons), grew up. He showed her where John Grisham's and Rita May Brown's farms were, and where The Grey Ghost, John Mosby's home, was. He described the areas around C'ville where Sissy Spacek and Howie Long lived, and where Meriwether Lewis and Jack Jouett grew up. He couldn't shut up about Charlottesville. He told her where the woman who claimed to be Anastasia had lived, where John Kluge used to live, and Miller's on the downtown mall where Dave

Matthews bartended, and Edgar Allen Poe's room on the lawn at the University. He hoped he hadn't yakked too much, but he had to add that Tami Hoag, John Casey, and Jan Karon lived in the area. They had lunch at Hamilton's on the downtown mall.

Remembering the ride home, Sedalia told him Troop had found a fresh trail up behind T. Wayne's home that he wanted to check out. She said she had tried to persuade Troop not to go alone, but she was afraid he was going anyway. She said Troop believed T. Wayne had never left the area and might be hiding out at the old abandoned farmstead behind his home on Squire Mountain. She said Troop knew, like the rest of us, that when T. Wayne's wife used her power of attorney and left him, she took all his money. He was probably broke, and had come back and was hiding out in that old barn and was going back and forth to his home at night to get food. Clay and Sedalia both worried that something bad might happen. Sedalia said she would check on Troop the next day to make sure he was okay.

When Sedalia went to check the next day she learned the terrible truth. She called out to him and saw him holding onto a chair trying to come to the door. His hands were scorched and swollen and his face, ears, and neck were blistered. His eyebrows and most of his hair were singed and, speaking in a whisper, he told her, "I found T. Wayne." She then learned that Troop had followed the trail to the front door of the barn, had tried to slip quietly inside, but the old boards leading up to the loft creaked and must have alerted T. Wayne. T. Wayne hit him from behind, knocking him unconscious. He then tied his hands and feet with binder twine and set the barn on fire. Troop awoke to the smell of smoke, intense heat and the loud crackle of flames that had engulfed the barn. He managed to free his feet by raking the binder twine over a rusty nail on the wall. He was then able to stand and run against the side of the barn. On his second try he had to run through the flames. He crashed through the burning boards and fell about fifteen feet to the ground. From there he somehow managed to struggle home. Sedalia called Clay and Robert and they took Troop to the emergency room at Lynchburg General. They treated the burns, gave him ointment and gave him some shots for infection.

CHAPTER 17

Health nuts are going to feel stupid one day—
lying in hospitals dying of nothing.
—Redd Foxx

Going to Troop's place the next day to check on the animals was lonely without Sedalia. Buckshot and Ruby met him with tails wagging. Feeding the chickens was easy and Millie and Mabeline were appreciative. Clay sat on the porch and relaxed after feeding the dogs. He thought about Junior, his father Earl, and his mother Betty Lou. People said Earl was passive and even submissive where his wife and Junior were concerned, but was dictatorial and over-bearing toward others. People who worked for him in his trucking business said he was short tempered, rude and hard to live with; none of them really liked him. Somehow, Earl had built what seemed to be a very profitable operation in a tough business. Still sitting on the porch with his legs dangling down, he felt Buckshot touching his back when he plopped down behind him. Also beside him, Ruby put her head on his leg and looked in his face. She looked worried as if to ask where is Troop? Both looked lonely; they probably missed Blue, too. Clay thought about what animals felt. He knew they grieved and he knew they had instincts about things humans don't understand. In the tsunami in Indonesia, flamingos left hours before the waves came. Water buffalos stampeded inland. The elephants were restless and almost all the dogs went to higher ground. A geologist in San Francisco predicted earthquakes based on looking at the number of lost cats and dogs in the classified ads. He said when the normal number of missing animals shot up, an earthquake could be coming.

Clay figured Sedalia should be back from her raptor rehabilitation class in Waynesboro by six so he called, but there was no answer. He also tried her cell phone again, but there was no answer. Oh well, maybe some of the group went to dinner after class. He tried again at 7:30 and there was no answer. Clay began to worry. He tried her cell phone again and left a message to call him. Sedalia didn't like to drive after dark, especially on a curvy country road like 151. She could have cut through on Route 6 near Nellysford and come out at Woods Mill on Route 29, or she could have stayed on 151 over Brent's Mountain, which had more curves.

Maybe she was tired and didn't feel like answering the phone, so he rode to her house to make sure she was okay.

When he got there he didn't see her car. No lights were on except the dusk to dawn light between the house and the shed. The dogs were glad to see him, but they looked apprehensive, even concerned. There was nothing to do but go back home and worry.

The phone rang around 9 o'clock and the caller ID flashed University Hospital. Clay nervously pressed the "talk" button and said hello.

"Is this Clay Hollister?"

"Yes."

"We found your name and phone number in the purse of a patient we recently admitted, a Ms. Sedalia Daniels. Do you know her?"

"Yes, is she all right? What happened?"

"She was in an automobile accident going up Brent's Mountain. I don't know the details."

"Is she hurt? Is she okay?"

"She's pretty banged up—cuts and bruises, she seems in shock. We're not sure if there are any broken bones. Do you know if she has any immediate family? Your name was the only one listed to notify in case of emergency."

"I think she has some cousins out west, but I don't know their names or how to reach them. I think I need to come to Charlottesville. I know where the hospital is."

"She's in Emergency now; she may be in another area by the time you get here."

Clay quickly changed clothes and got in the Jeep. Traffic was light on Route 29 to Charlottesville. He set the Jeep on cruise control and put in a Mozart CD. The stream of consciousness of recent events began to fly through his mind and what had happened to Troop; what had caused Mack's death; what had caused Sedalia's wreck? Something strange and sinister was going on with Rip's brother Easel, and why had he started coming to Rucker's? And sooner or later Rip's sons, Axle and Rance, and Earl's son, Junior, were going to cross the line into serious trouble if they hadn't done so already.

His main concern now, though, was Sedalia. He realized how often he thought of her, and how lost he would feel without her. He still didn't know how she felt about him, but his name as the only person to contact in an emergency had to mean something.

His mind skipped to finding another horse to replace Blackjack. Horses like company and Pepper looked lonesome. He knew of one horse that had a cat for a buddy. The cat lived in the barn and sometimes got on the horse's back, curled up and went to sleep. Studs and high-strung horses often had a mule, donkey or even a goat, dog or cat for a companion. They became difficult and tense if they were separated from their companion. Anyway, the horse sale in Lexington was coming up soon, plus the economy was creating horses for adoption because the owners couldn't afford to keep them.

By then he was entering Charlottesville and he took the first exit after going under I-64. He turned on Fountaine Ave, which turned into Jefferson Park Ave until he saw the Emergency Room sign at Lee Street. He parked in the garage opposite the emergency room.

A receptionist said Sedalia was still there. When he walked in, her whole upper body seemed to be in bandages. Her face was swollen and he could see stitches on her left cheek, chin and across her nose. She looked groggy, but there was a flicker of recognition. Clay took her hand and bent close as she tried to speak, "I was run off the road coming up Brent's Mountain," she whispered. He could see it hurt to speak.

"Don't talk; there'll be lots of time to talk later. I'll take care of the animals, so don't worry about them."

It seemed she tried to smile.

A nurse came in to check her and gave her a shot. The nurse nodded to Clay to follow her out of the room.

"I think she'll be okay, but she'll be in a lot of pain for a few days. I gave her the shot to relax her and help her sleep. We'll monitor everything through the night, but she'll be out of it till morning. You may want to go home and come back tomorrow."

"I guess you're right. I'll stick around a few minutes till she goes to sleep. Tell her when she wakes up I'll be back."

"Sure, you might bring her a housecoat if you think of it."

Clay went back and stood by the bed and held her hand. He felt her squeeze it. He watched her eyes flutter and felt her grip loosen as she dozed off.

CHAPTER 18

Church Bulletin:
Miss Charlene Morris sang "I Will Not Pass This Way Again,"
giving obvious pleasure to the congregation.

It was after midnight when he left. The drive back was filled with thoughts about the wreck, how it happened, how long it would take for her to recover. It dawned on him that he now needed to not only take care of his animals, but her animals along with Troop's. Maybe he could call Henry and get her thoughts on how to take care of her when she comes home, especially if she is unable to bathe or dress herself.

He went to Sedalia's early the next morning and went inside. Luckily, she didn't lock her doors. He found some dog food, went to the shed and found some feed for the ducks and geese. There was only one bird, a red-tail hawk that she was rehabilitating. He didn't know what to feed it so he refilled the water cup; he would ask Sedalia what to feed it. Feeling awkward, he went into her bedroom and managed to find a housecoat. He called Robert on his cell phone and told him what had happened. Clay told him he would call later when he knew more about Sedalia's condition. He stopped at Rucker's and filled Cecil in.

Sedalia had been put in a private room. She seemed disoriented, but awake. She was heavily sedated, but she recognized him.

"Hi, Clay," was all she managed.

He took her hand and told her he had been by the house and that all the animals were fine. He asked if she felt like telling him what to feed the hawk.

The nurse came in and gave her some pills and another shot. She then told Sedalia, "You're one lucky lady, you've got a lot of cuts and bruises from the air bag, but no broken bones except one fractured rib. You're going to be sore, it will hurt to take deep breaths, but in two to three weeks you'll be almost good as new."

A doctor came in with another nurse and told Clay to wait in the hall, that he'd only be a few minutes.

When Clay went back in, Sedalia was trying to speak and Clay, seeing it was painful, told her not to talk.

"No," she whispered, "I've got to tell you I recognized the driver that ran me off the road."

Clay was stunned.

"Are you sure?"

"It was one of those brothers that drive those big black pickups—one of Rip's boys—the one with the missing front tooth. I went off the road and down a steep ravine just before where the guardrail starts at the first switchback. It's the last thing I remember. I could see him through the windshield—he had an evil grin—like he wanted to hit me."

"Do you think he singled you out on purpose?"

"I doubt it. I think it could have been anyone. He had a wild, crazy look."

Seeing Sedalia was getting upset, he said, "That's unbelievable! But let's wait till you're feeling better; then we'll figure out what to do. I'm sure someone from the sheriff's office will be investigating the accident and will be in to talk to you." Clay added, "I know you're hurting, but I've got to ask you, what do I feed the hawk?"

Sedalia, showing pain, answered, "There's a small refrigerator in the feed room where I keep medicines and some dead mice. There should be several in the plastic bowl with the blue lid in the refrigerated part. Give her two or three and take some out of the carton in the freezer and put them in the refrigerator tray to thaw for late tomorrow."

Clay stayed most of the day and watched as she drifted in and out of sleep. Finally, he knew he had to leave to get back in time to feed their animals and check in with Henry.

On the way home his memory became more morbid when he crossed the Rockfish River at Woods Mill. The nearby Davis Creek area was where so many died. He recalled the terrible flood of Hurricane Camille in August of '69. Around thirty inches of rain fell in a five-hour period. They say it was the country's first category-five hurricane. At least 125 Nelson County people died that night and 52 of them were from the Davis Creek area. One hundred ninety-three houses were destroyed in the county and 70 more were damaged. Twenty-three major bridges were lost along with 67 smaller ones.

Thinking back, Clay imagined the terror of suddenly being swept away. Most of the victims died from crushing earth slides of trees, boulders and mud, or from drowning. There were few injuries—you either died or survived. The second highest loss of life of 22 occurred at Massies Mill and the next highest of 10 was at Tyro, a short distance away.

Some of the stories told were incredible. A farmer at Woods Mill, who was moving his cattle to high ground, said he could see headlights off in the distance where the bridge on Route 29 crossed the Rockfish River. He said he would see headlights and suddenly they disappeared because there was no longer a bridge. Someone saw a tractor-trailer go in and it was never found. Witnesses said birds drowned while roosting in trees and people caught out in the downpour had to hold their hand over their nose to breathe. The Roseland post office sign was later found over 200 miles away in Hampton.

Today, the area is verdant and serene, but on that night the rain saturated the earth and whole sides of mountains slid away. The slides piled up behind jams of logs and rocks until the tremendous pressure of the onrushing water caused the whole mess to explode. Witnesses said it sounded like a huge bomb.

It was getting late when Clay pulled into Sedalia's yard. The animals were getting used to his vehicles so there was less commotion. After a light feeding of the animals, he fed the hawk some of the dead mice. He then ran water to refill the tub in the yard.

At home, after petting Jake and Rita, he checked his messages. His only message was from Henry wanting him to call her about Sedalia. She left her cell phone number.

"Hey, Henry, just got back from Charlottesville and got your message."

"How's our girl doing?"

"She's pretty banged up, but the outlook is positive. She told me one of Rip's boys—I think his name is Axle—deliberately ran her off the road on the other side of Brent's Mountain."

"I think I know the one you mean—that whole bunch is trash. I'd like to shoot those two with my tranquilizer gun—when they woke up they'd be able to sing soprano."

"Henry, you've got a mean streak."

"Not really; it's just that the reduction in testosterone has a wonderful calming effect on the male animal."

"Seriously, Henry, I'm thinking they will release her in a few days, and I don't know if she can take care of herself, like bathing, dressing, going to the bathroom."

"Don't worry; when you find out when, just let me know. There are several local women I can get to stay with her."

"Thanks, you're a lifesaver. Incidentally, I've thought of coming to you instead of my town doctor. A friend of a friend goes to see his vet for all the normal stuff. Y'all use the same medicines.

You could give me a shot of 'bute' for my back and cortisone for my shoulder. Just set me up as 'Fido' in your system. Who would know?"

"Hang up, Clay. You might be recording this just to get me in trouble. Let me know when you find out about Sedalia. Bye."

CHAPTER 19

It is possible for two people to know less about a subject
than one of them alone.

The next morning Clay stopped in at Rucker's and could see Burl had the group enthralled in a story—one Clay was sure he had heard, but it turned out he hadn't.

Burl nodded to Clay and began.

"This ain't no story—this is a quiz."

"A quiz?" asked Clay.

"Yeah, Cecil was talking the other day about early moonshine runners becoming great NASCAR drivers. Y'all are always going on 'bout Jimmy Johnson, Kyle Busch, Jeff Gordon and so on. I'm wondering if any of you know who was the best driver ever?"

Before he could finish, Bill piped up, "Hell, that's easy—Dale Earnhardt."

"Maybe, the 'Intimidator' was one of the best. Did you hear about that race at Bristol in '95? Dale was trying to get by Terry Labonte on the final lap so Dale gave him a little bump, hoping he'd spin out. Only, it didn't work. Terry somehow stayed on the track and crossed the finish line going backwards ahead of Dale. They say he's the only NASCAR driver to win a race going backwards. But you didn't let me finish. The fellow I'm thinking 'bout was a moonshine runner and earned his stripes on back roads and dirt tracks. When my man raced, the biggest bets were on who was going to come in second."

"How about Richard Petty, or his dad, Lee?"

"Nope, don't know if they hauled moonshine, but I don't think they were as good as my man. My man is out of North

Carolina. He's a big, amiable fellow off the track, but other drivers said what put the fear of God in them was to see him coming up in their rearview mirror. Like other moonshine drivers, he knew how to do a one-eighty at full speed. If he was being chased by a revenue agent, or saw a roadblock ahead, he'd throw it into second gear, jerk the wheel sharply to the left and jam the accelerator to the floor and do a complete 'about-face' and roar back from where he came."

"Sounds like Curtis Turner."

"He was a great one and he did haul moonshine, but he's from Virginia."

"Anyway, some claim this man figured out drafting. In one race with Fireball Roberts, he had the slower car, but he found if he got right behind Fireball's Pontiac, he could not only keep up with him, but both cars went faster. Also, he figured out something else. In those days everyone was sliding into the curves on the dirt tracks. He developed a technique of turning his wheels sharply to the left going into the curve, so instead of using the slide for braking, he could accelerate halfway through the curve and come out like a shot."

Someone chimed in, "How about the old guy, Mark Martin?"

"No, it wasn't him, but he's one of my favorites. They say when he was driving the Viagra car, he kept having trouble with the hood flying up."

The group laughed, but sat spellbound, scratching their heads.

"One last tidbit—it ain't really a clue, but he was such a thorn in the side of those revenue agents, they tried every way they could think of to catch him. They came up with what seemed like a foolproof plan. They knew the nights he was likely to make a run and the road he was likely to take, so they set up a barricade at the far end of a narrow bridge. They were sure there was no way out.

"On that night, they heard his high-powered engine coming down the road. Then, just as he was approaching the bridge, they heard a siren and saw the flashing red light through the grill. Thinking it was another agent in hot pursuit, they scrambled to move the barricade and scattered as he roared through.

"Damn, there he goes again! He's done gone and put a siren and flashing red light in his car!"

Professor Willis spoke up. "You're talking about Junior Johnson."

Burl looked bewildered. "How the hell would a college professor know that?"

"Well, he's an astute businessman and a shrewd investor. You can now buy his legal moonshine at many Virginia ABC stores. It's sold under the 'Midnight Moon' label. And, by the way, you don't have to be a redneck to enjoy stock car racing. Gotta go, or I'll be late for class."

Still puzzled, Burl changed the subject. "Remind me to tell y'all sometime 'bout how we got rid of that wild outlaw motorcycle gang that used to come up here from Richmond. They came up every Fourth of July week and raised hell up at Wildcat Falls. One last thing I want to say about moonshine is they say Wilkes County, North Carolina, was the moonshine capital of America, but Franklin County here in Virginia claims it's the moonshine capital of the world."

Several disagreed with Burl's choice. Bull blurted out, "All that stuff about Junior Johnson is bull crap (except he didn't say crap). Best driver ever was Bill Elliott." He stood up and walked out in a huff.

Cecil and Robert came over and asked about Troop and Sedalia. Clay said he believed there was some good news on Troop, and he felt Sedalia would come home in a day or two. Cecil went to wait on a customer and Robert said, "Looks like you got your hands full looking after Sedalia's animals plus your own. I'll be glad to look after Troop's dogs and livestock."

"You sure you don't mind?"

"Hell, Clay, Troop's one of my best friends. He's good company—doesn't run his mouth and he's comfortable to be around. I've also been checking in on Lula, so it won't be no trouble to go by Troop's place. Lula's still got some of her family with her and she seems to 'preciate me coming by, but if anyone mentions Mack, she breaks down."

Clay followed, "What happened to Troop and Mack and Sedalia has me really worked up. I'm sure Rip's outfit and Junior are tied in with the wreck and the beating. Even if Troop regains consciousness, he might not know who hit him."

"I agree," said Robert, "and in Sedalia's case, even if the police question Axle, it'll be his word against hers. He ran her off the road, but he didn't hit her, so there's no evidence and no witnesses."

Clay responded, "I've got an idea. You know the one they call 'Snake'? He's got a drinking problem, but otherwise he's okay. We speak in passing from time to time. I might ask him to keep his ears open down at the *He Ain't Here* bar. I'm thinking Rance, Axle, and Junior might start bragging after a few beers, and I'm pretty sure Snake is not friends with them."

"Good idea. I know the police wrote up the wrecks, did measurements, took pictures and so forth, but I want to go by both Mack's and Sedalia's wreck sites and see if I can find any clues. I also plan to go by Jamerson's Wrecking and take a close look at Mack's truck. He might have been sideswiped by whoever ran him off the road. There might be some scrapes on the bumper or the mirror or on the side of the truck body.

"I'm also going to check around Troop's place and see if I can find a path through the woods where he somehow dragged himself or crawled back to the road. Maybe I can backtrack to where it happened. I doubt there's anything to see where Sedalia wrecked."

Clay gave Robert a sly, quizzical look and commented, "You do have a knack for that kind of stuff. See ya in a couple of days."

CHAPTER 20

A person will believe 90 percent of what is whispered to them.

The next few days were a blur for Clay. He visited Troop, and his nurse said the swellings were going down and she had seen some more finger and foot movements. She said his eyes had stayed open a little longer.

Henry took an afternoon off and rode with him to Charlottesville to bring Sedalia home. She said she had found two local ladies to take turns staying with her. After they got Sedalia settled in, he went to Rucker's with her grocery list. She had slowly but steadily improved and was beginning to show signs of her normal upbeat personality.

Clay got another call from Troop's nurse two nights later—the nurse he originally thought was a hard-nose "Nurse Ratched," like in *One Flew Over the Cuckoo's Nest*, but who turned out to be a soft-hearted teddy bear.

"Guess what!" she exclaimed. "Our boy kept his eyes open most of the day!"

"No kidding."

"Yep, he doesn't know where he is. He keeps looking round the room and at the ceiling and at me. It looked like he wanted to speak, but nothing came out."

"That's great news! I'm coming to see him in the morning."

"If I'm not around, ask for Sara—we both have a thing about Troop. Bye."

Clay, trying not to get overly excited, called Sedalia. She sounded a little sedated, but alert. Luckily, he caught her between painkiller naps.

"Good news—Troop's nurse just called and said he'd opened his eyes today. I'm going to see him in the morning."

"That is wonderful news—wish I could go with you."

"I wish you felt like going. I'll call Robert to see if he wants to come along. I shouldn't get my hopes up, but I can't help it. I know you don't feel like talking, so I'll shut up, but I'll give you a full report when I get back tomorrow."

"Thanks. Be sure to tell him I love him and can't wait to see him."

When Clay called, Robert sounded enthusiastic and said he would share some interesting news when they met. Clay suggested they meet at Rucker's the next morning at 9:00. Then Clay said, "I'd like to run something by you—it might sound crazy, but what do you think about asking Dew to ride along with us?"

Robert hesitated, then said, "That might be good therapy for Troop and Dew, but I doubt Gladys will let him go."

"Well, it won't hurt to ask. I'll ride up this afternoon and see what she says. I'll call you back."

Robert laughed and said, "The three of us might turn a few heads—it might be an interesting day."

When Robert went to see Gladys and Dew, he told them Troop was awake and doing better. He told her that he and Robert were going to visit Troop in the morning and wondered if Dew could come along. Gladys was shaking her head before he finished asking. "No, no, no," she said. "He don't have nothin' to wear and them people will make fun of him."

Clay responded, "Troop and Dew are good buddies and it might help Troop to see Dew—and nobody is going to make fun of him with Robert and me along."

Gladys was saying, "I still don't think it's such a good idea," when Dew broke in, "Want to see Troop—Troop best friend—me want to go!"

He said it in such a way that Gladys just stared. Hearing how determined he spoke, she sputtered, "Well, if you want to go that bad, I reckon it'll be okay—I'll wash that best thing of yours and you need to wash your hair and wear them good tennis shoes."

Surprised, Clay said he'd pick him up around a quarter to nine. When he got home he called Robert and told him the good news.

When Clay picked up Dew, he had washed his long stringy blond hair, had on a clean sack dress, and was grinning from ear to ear. Gladys just shook her head and said, "I don't know—y'all take good care of 'em."

Clay picked up Robert and the three sat in the front seat of the pickup with Dew in the middle. On the ride to Lynchburg, Dew was all eyes—trying to see everything on both sides of the road. Dew probably hadn't been to Lynchburg more than three or four times in his life.

The stares started when they got out in the parking lot. Robert put on his stoic face when they walked in the front entrance. Nobody was going to mess with Robert when he was wearing his stoic face. Clay knew Robert could switch it off and turn on a smile that would melt butter.

As they were walking in, Clay had to stop momentarily to tie his shoe and overheard a visitor comment to his friend, "That's the ugliest woman I've ever seen."

At 6'4" with long blond hair, hairy legs above his high top tennis shoes and wearing a feed sack dress, Clay wondered what people thought. Actually, his outfit was an improvement over the usual hospital garb. They probably thought he was being escorted to the psychiatric ward. Dew, showing his usual gentle disposition, walked slightly stooped. He was also taking it all in like a kid in a toy store.

They were getting ready to go into Troop's room when Nurse Sara came up. Having seen it all, she took no special notice of Dew.

She explained before they entered, "Don't expect too much—he's still not totally with us. Don't be surprised if he doesn't recognize you."

As they slowly entered the room, Troop seemed traumatized. There was no sign of recognition. Dew, on the other hand, seemed in shock seeing all the bandages and hanging bottles with tubes attached to a needle in his arms. Clay and Robert spoke softly and told Troop his dogs and animals were fine and that Sedalia sends her love.

Dew had slowly moved closer and reached over and touched Troop's hand. For the first time, Troop seemed to recognize Dew. A slight smile flickered as their eyes met. Troop closed his fingers around Dew's hand. There was a connection and they all saw it.

Soon it was time to leave. Reluctantly, Dew removed his hand.

Clay suggested they stop at McDonald's for lunch. They ordered Dew a Big Mac meal, which he tasted apprehensively and then ate heartily. They topped it off with a hot fudge sundae. His manners were not exactly Emily Post, but he wasn't sloppy either. Dew had seldom eaten store bought food, but they could tell he enjoyed it.

On the way home Robert told Clay what he had found.

"I spent day before yesterday backtracking Troop's route. Sure 'nuf, just up from where they found him, I could still see where the leaves were scratched up where he and Blue tumbled down the bank. From there he and Blue left an easy trail to follow. I believe Troop must have crawled a good part of the way. Their trail led up the ridge and over two high ridges and then along a side ridge that probably touched the tip end of Rip's large tract. I found an area where the leaves flattened out and beside it were signs where it looked like someone had struggled and floundered around. There seemed to be a few small specks of blood, which probably belonged to Troop and Blue. It's hard to imagine how anyone beaten up that badly could have traveled that far. It's a miracle. From where I found the leaves, I could look down on a well-worn path. That path might be the one Rip's brother and his guards patrol. I could see a 'No Trespassin' sign beside the path. I still can't believe he traveled that far. It's no wonder his hands and knees were raw and bloody."

Clay responded, "Son of a gun. It's a wonder he and Blue are alive."

"Right, and yesterday I went by Jamerson's Wrecking Yard and looked over what was left of the truck. I found a suspicious fresh streak of black paint. It was on the metal strip on the side of the floor bed of the body on the driver's side. It could have come from sideswiping the mirror on Junior's Mustang. Also, at the wreck scene there were small slivers of glass in the road, like broken glass from a mirror. His Mustang is a bright candy apple red, but his side mirrors are black. It's a long shot, but I want to get a good look at Junior's car the first chance I get."

"Robert, you amaze me. I think you're on to something."

Dew sat quietly while Clay and Robert talked. After letting Robert off at Rucker's, he took Dew home. Gladys seemed greatly relieved and Dew was beaming and exclaimed, "Good day!"

CHAPTER 21

A sharp tongue and a dull brain
are often found in the same head.

The next morning when Clay stopped at Rucker's, all heads turned to hear about Troop. The group wanted to know all the details which Robert and Clay gladly provided. Nothing, however, was said about what Robert had found. The news put everyone in high spirits even though there were worries about Troop regaining his mental faculties. He told them about his reaction to Dew.

In a lighthearted mood, Bull spoke. "Bet Ole Troop ain't too happy with them nurses messin' with his body. Doubt he's ever been naked round nobody—especially round women, or people he don't know."

From there the conversation went downhill. It sparked a discussion about lack of privacy and personal ailments. It's odd how someone can make an unrelated comment and turn a conversation in a completely different direction.

Burl complained about his ailment of having to get up to pee several times a night. Woodrow followed, "Me too, my problem is pressure. Back when I was young I could pee on the campfire seven feet away. If I tried it now, I'd have to be so close I'd roast the wrong weenie."

The group chuckled and Bill Ware added, "Burl, next time you get your VA physical, make sure they check your prostate."

"I'm not sure they do that anymore unless your PSA is off."

"You can tell 'em to do it anyway."

Clay chimed in. "Both my local doctor and my VA doctor are women and I still get squeamish when some things are checked.

The first time it happened I was getting my physical at the VA in Salem. My doctor then was a man, but that day he had a UVA medical student observing. While the doctor was briefly out of the room she and I were having a pleasant conversation about the goings on in Charlottesville and UVA. She was young, interesting and attractive. I thought surely he would tell her to leave the room. Instead, he said to me, "Drop your trousers and your shorts and bend over the bed." It was the most embarrassed I'd been in a long time because the young lady was seated directly behind me at butt level."

Cecil, who was temporarily listening in, commented, "How do you think women feel when they go to a male gynecologist?"

Bill interrupted and said, "I saw a decal on a Harley helmet that read, 'I'm not a trained gynecologist, but I'll be glad to take a look.'" The group laughed, but Bull didn't seem to get it.

Robert followed, "I felt the same way the first time a woman checked my prostate. Luckily, she had a good sense of humor. Seeing my embarrassment, she quipped, 'Just remember, we women have smaller fingers.'" Cecil said, "I've heard prostate surgery can change your sex life." Clay added, "One man I know had the operation. He said he could still hear the orchestra but not the trumpet section."

Woodrow interrupted, "Prostate ain't nothing. A colonoscopy is the worst invasion of privacy there is. The women that prepped me, though, looked tough as nails—reminded me of mechanics workin' on my truck. They must see some terrible sights. How'd you like lookin' at people's butts all day for a livin'? Anyway, the thought of it is worse than the actual."

"It won't so bad. Oh, and just be sure you're in running distance of a bathroom when you have to drink that stuff the day before," commented Burl. "There's so much sexual and body function stuff on TV, there's no privacy left. Gettin' patted down at the airport is a walk in the park. One fellow said it felt so good he asked them to do it again. And what difference does it really make if it's the back of the hand or the palm?"

As often happened, someone mentioned sex with the usual Cialis and Viagra comments. Cecil, however, brought the conversation back to semi-respectable by saying, "Getting laid at our age is an incomplete sentence—it ought to be getting laid to rest."

Clay bought a BBQ sandwich to go and a half-gallon of 2 percent milk. Bull once said he won't going to buy no 2 percent milk because it was only 2 percent milk.

CHAPTER 22

If Roosevelt were alive today,
he would turn over in his grave.
—Samuel Goldwyn

Sedalia lay in bed partially sedated, yet still aware of aches and pains. Grateful her injuries weren't worse, she, however, seethed with anger and frustration. The detective from the Nelson County Sheriff's office had just left. She suspected what he was going to say by his demeanor and body language. She knew there probably wouldn't be any arrest or charges. He knew she was telling the truth, but he knew it would be her word against Axle's and there were no tire marks, or witnesses, or other evidence. The detective said just filing a complaint might cause problems from Axle.

He told her the brothers were well known to the police departments in Amherst, Nelson, Somerset and Albemarle counties. There were also records across the mountains in Rockbridge and Augusta counties. The charges were mostly aggravated assault, reckless driving and barroom fights—things their lawyer could get reduced or dismissed. Axle was the main instigator, but his brother Rance was a willing participant. Rance pretty much did what Axle told him. Locals could tell Rance had a mental deficiency, but his constant goofy grin somewhat lessened fears of a malicious nature. Cecil said he was one French fry shy of a Happy Meal. Rumor had it that as a child he liked to pull wings off of butterflies and shoot songbirds with his 22. He usually had several days of thick beard growth and always chewed tobacco. The juice trickled from the corners of his mouth down through the stubble, which he rubbed off with the back of his hand or on his shirtsleeve. Most thought he was harmless, but Sedalia said he made her uncomfortable the way he stared.

Even though Sedalia knew she would probably be on Axle's hit list after the detective talked with him, she couldn't help fantasizing about how to get even. The detective told her to tell her insurance agent to have their adjuster give him a call.

Sedalia's dark mood shifted with Clay's entrance and the good news about Troop was just what she needed. Clay said the nurse believed he would be coming out of it in a day or two. Sedalia was ecstatic and Clay's description of the way people looked at Dew at the hospital and how Troop responded to seeing him was icing on the cake. Then he brought her up to date on what Robert had found. He told her about him finding the streak of black paint and mirror shards and how he had tracked Troop and Blue's trail the long distance to the edge of Rip's land.

Sedalia's mood then shifted again. She went from happy to detached and somber. Clay sat and wondered what was coming next. When she started talking, her voice began changing. She seemed to drift into a stream of consciousness. Her voice was deeper and raspy.

"Lying here the past few days I've been seeing Troop's, Mack's, and my experience. It's very strange, yet somehow connected. We know about Rip's boys and Junior, but there is more that is puzzling."

Clay sat on the edge of his chair. "I've been seeing Earl Dooley and Ole Rip somehow connected. Yet, I've never heard they even know each other. How could Earl have made so much money so fast? I've heard trucking is a thin-margin business. Something just doesn't add up."

Her voice kept getting deeper and her eyes took on a glazed look. At times her comments didn't seem connected. "Why would Rip's brother be hanging 'round Rucker's? He never did before. And how can Ole Rip's boys afford those big pickups and race cars? There's no doubt Troop's beating came from Rip's clan. Ole Rip could be making moonshine, growing marijuana, or whatever. Who knows? Why would he patrol his land so close? Troop was probably trying to keep up with Blue. That coon must have run a long way. I'm thinking Ole Rip and Earl might have some business connections like hauling moonshine and bringing in supplies for the operation. I've been having strange dreams. Maybe it's the pain medicine, but some of my dreams are surreal. Last night there were angels fighting devils. The devils threw tri-pointed spears, but the angels were too quick. I don't know what it means, but I get the feeling I'm missing something."

Sedalia then seemed to shake it off and came back. "Sorry, I didn't mean to go on so."

Clay could only say, "What you said makes sense. Robert and I feel the same way, but we hadn't made any connection between Earl and Ole Rip. You keep thinking and we'll keep you posted on anything we hear. I'll feed the animals before I go. The cows still have most of the large round hay bale."

Sedalia added, "Feed the hawk a couple of more dead mice. She's almost ready for the live ones. I need to be sure she has retained her killer instincts before she can be released." She then added, "Thanks for everything, Clay—don't know what I'd do without you."

Clay almost made a similar response, but instead answered, "No problem, you know I like being outdoors and feeding things. Take care."

On his way home and while he was doing his own chores, Clay reflected about what Sedalia had said. He still couldn't see a connection between Earl and Ole Rip, but her intuition had been on target in their previous experience with T. Wayne. His thoughts caused Clay to recall the final episode involving T. Wayne.

After his first near death from the barn fire, Troop told Robert he believed T. Wayne was still around and had gone further up in the mountains and might be hiding out in a cave on Squires Mountain. State and local police were searching every nook and cranny and newspapers and TV were reporting the search. The law was finally pursuing T. Wayne for the murder of Sally Jessup. Robert tried to tell the officer in charge about where T. Wayne might be hiding, but his efforts were caustically rebuffed. The commander told him in no uncertain terms that his ideas were not needed and the locals should stay out of the way. Incensed, Robert decided he would follow Troop's directions and check out the cave.

After making up a story for Corine, he sat out to make the long climb just before nightfall. He managed to spot the cave opening as darkness was closing in. His plan was to first yell for T. Wayne to come out with his hands up. Robert yelled three times for T. Wayne to come out. When that didn't work, plan B was to set a fire and push the burning embers to the opening with a long, forked stick. After getting the fire started, he put a bandana over his nose and cautiously pushed the fire close to the opening. Finally, T. Wayne came tumbling out, coughing and gasping for air. Robert immediately pounced on his back, tied his hands behind him and tied on a blindfold. He then said, "All right, you son of a bitch. We're going to walk down this mountain. You do what I say and maybe you won't fall off a cliff, but it wouldn't bother me none if you did."

They stumbled, slipped and slid down the steep descent. T. Wayne had a few bad falls. Soon they hit the old logging road and followed it to Robert's truck. He lowered the tailgate and calmly said, "This is for what you did to Troop," then hit him with his pistol, knocking him unconscious. He laid him in the truck bed and wrapped a heavy old horse blanket round him and tucked it underneath. Robert then drove him to Raeford's where many of the search team were having a late dinner. He spotted the large black unmarked police cruiser with all the antennas that he assumed belonged to the commander. He heaved T. Wayne's unconscious body across its hood and slowly drove away. The next day the TV and newspaper headlined the miraculous capture and arrest.

CHAPTER 23

When you talk to God, they call it prayer.
When God talks to you, they say you're crazy.

Winter was now flying by. A period followed when Clay and Robert took care of Troop's, Sedalia's and their own animals. Troop had been transferred to a rehab ward where he steadily improved. The time came for his release and he reluctantly agreed to stay with Clay until he was strong enough to move back to his cabin. On the day of his release, Clay went to pick him up. His two favorite nurses had fixed him a small cake with a single candle and were giving him a farewell party. They both teared up and Troop looked like he didn't quite know how to respond. He seemed embarrassed. With his head slightly tucked, he told them he 'preciated all they'd done.

Clay had put a single bed in a converted storage room downstairs beside the kitchen. He added a bedside table, lamp and comfortable chair along with a small TV that had previously been in the kitchen. In the hospital Troop had gotten hooked on TV. Never having owned one before, he was fascinated by all the programs. He especially liked *The Andy Griffith Show*, old westerns, hunting and fishing and rodeo programs. He did have a radio in his cabin, but Clay believed he had mostly listened to the news, weather and country music.

With the remote control in hand, he stayed entertained for hours. He could make his way to the bathroom and the kitchen table. He kept telling Clay he was sorry 'bout being a burden. Clay assured him he enjoyed his company.

Robert came over the first night and kept the mood cheerful and entertaining. They talked about hunting and fishing memories and Gladys and Dew and all the gang at Rucker's. Sedalia was also getting around and beginning to feel comfortable with just the stockman's cane Clay had given her. On her first visit she brought a large pot of vegetable beef soup, ham biscuits, rice pudding, cornbread muffins and a chocolate pie.

Troop, who wasn't much of a talker, would listen and make brief comments. They could tell the visits were appreciated, and that the local news and how Blue and his other animals were getting along were his main interests.

There were times when he complained of headaches and dizziness. He still had a short attention span and occasionally slurred words, but he was eating well and getting stronger. He seemed to have total recall of everything up to the beating, but no memory of anything afterwards until waking up in the hospital. He was troubled and disturbed as to why anyone would have beaten him. Clay promised he would take him to visit his cabin on the first warm day as soon as he was strong enough. Clay could sense his anxious anticipation of being reunited with his closest companions.

One night while they were sitting around talking, Clay cautiously mentioned that sometimes when a person had almost died they had strange visions. He mentioned this and asked Troop if he remembered anything unusual. There was a long silence and Clay wondered if he had gotten too personal. Finally, Troop said, "If I told you what I'd seen, you'd think I was crazy."

"No, I wouldn't. I've heard when someone has technically died they often go to a different place and sometimes see their parents and close friends who have died. They say it's very pleasant."

Again, silence, then, "Yeah, something like that. I seemed to float up and look down and I seen me and Blue lying in that ditch, and I was wonderin' why we was lying there. Saw the same thing in the hospital. Saw them nurses and doctor workin' on me. It won't painful."

Clay wondered what else he felt and was afraid to push it, but Troop continued, "I felt real good. I felt safe and peaceful. It was springtime. I was in a nice, grassy place. There was birds 'n flowers by a clear stream. Then my mama and daddy and grandma came out of a bright light. They was smilin' and happy and told me everything was fine. There was also a bright spirit there, like an angel—no one I could touch. She said she was my guide and said not to worry. She told me my time had not come and that I needed to go back because there were things I still needed to do. I didn't want to come back, but she said I had to, and that we would meet again when the time was right. Them who met me seemed to understand. They drifted away, smilin' and I knew I'd see 'em again."

Troop seemed to enjoy the memory. Clay, not sure what to say, commented, "Sounds like you had a wonderful experience. I appreciate you telling me."

"Yeah, it was."

"I had a feeling you had experienced something. You have always been calm and easy going, but I felt there was something new about you. I can't explain it, like even more calm."

"Yeah, I do feel right peaceful."

"I know you are a Monacan Indian and I know your people were treated badly."

Troop answered, "My father used to talk about things that had been passed down from his ancestors. He said the Monacans ranged mostly in Central Virginia from the James River near Richmond to these Blue Ridge Mountains. Chief Powhatan's tribe was one of our enemies. Between them and the early settlers, we were pushed back and settled in this area. The center of our tribe now is Bear Mountain in Amherst County. Back then the counties and the state treated us like outcasts. My tribe has traveled a rough road."

Clay again was impressed with Troop's knowledge and how clearly he related it.

CHAPTER 24

Church Sign:
Catholic dogs go to heaven.
Presbyterian dogs can talk to their pastor.

When the sunny day arrived with the temperature in the forties, Clay helped Troop into the pickup. Clay put it in four-wheel drive and they bumped, slid and spun up the steep entrance to Troop's cabin. Ruby and Buckshot came barking and running with tails wagging. Troop rolled down his window and when Buckshot recognized him, he went into a frenzy. He began bounding and turning in circles and trying to jump through the window. Ruby came around and joined in the celebration. Clay went around and pushed the dogs aside to open the door. When Troop stepped down, they were trying to jump all over him. Clay held onto Troop until he collapsed on the ground in a pile with the dogs. It was hard to tell who was the happiest. They made their way toward the cabin. The next to see him was Mabeline, who gave several loud, elongated "hee haws" and looked like she might try to jump the fence. Millie also came to the fence and stuck her nose through the gate to meet Troop's hand.

Troop took a slow look around the barnyard, then inside the cabin. They sat on the front porch with a dog's head resting on each of Troop's legs. The next thing, which surprised Clay, was Troop slowly getting up and saying, "Got to go over and tell the bees I'm back."

The following day Clay took Troop to Rucker's. Clay made sure they arrived when most of the coffee crowd would be there. Clay had alerted Robert ahead of time so he was waiting. Burl,

Bull, Professor Willis, Woodrow, Walter, Bill and Cecil had also been told. It was a grand welcome and Troop was both thrilled and embarrassed. There was a flurry of questions and comments, but most of the banter was about how good it was to see Troop upright and becoming mobile again.

While everyone was talking, Cecil caught Clay's eye and motioned him aside. He said, "Our friend, 'Stinkbug' was in here a couple of days ago. Bull said Easel came up behind him while he was picking up some groceries. He said he smelled him before he saw him. Bull said Easel put the evil eye on him and roughly asked, 'How's that Indian doing?' Bull said he stared him right back and said, 'None of your goddamn business!' Bull said Easel looked startled, gave him a dirty look, and walked out." Cecil added, "Bull can put the evil eye on you as good as anybody."

Clay responded, "Good for Bull. We know there's a connection with Troop's beating and, yeah, Stinkbug is a good name."

As the conversation died down, Clay rejoined the group and commented he didn't want to wear Troop out so maybe they ought to go. Besides, he had told Troop he would take him by Gladys and Dew's house to see Blue.

Talk about a celebration. They say dogs can't smile, but Blue came close. He groveled first, and then lay on his back with all four feet pawing the air. Then he started nuzzling Troop and licking his hand, all the while making an excited whimper. He jumped up, putting both feet on Troop's shoulders and licked his face. In spite of a limp, Blue started jumping around and running back and forth as if to re-verify that Troop was real.

Gladys and Dew had come out on the porch to watch the show. Clay could see Dew was visibly excited but didn't know how to show it. Troop reached up to shake Dew's hand and Dew grabbed it with both hands. His facial expression said it all and Troop reflected back the same emotion. Gladys, as usual, exclaimed, "Lordy, lordy, lordy, Troop. It's mighty good to see ya."

It had been a good day. Gladys said later that Blue must have thought Troop was back at the cabin because he left on his own and stayed. Maybe he was also missing Ruby and Buckshot.

CHAPTER 25

Church Bulletin:
At the evening service tonight the sermon topic will be "What is Hell?"
Come early and listen to our choir practice.

Except for Troop's recent visit, Clay had not been to morning coffee for a while so he went in a little early. There were several locals plus Walter and Bill. Clay could tell Burl was on one of his favorite subjects of ghost stories.

Burl was saying, "Old Rex would go upstairs to bed with Grandma every night right at nine o'clock. Well, after Grandma died, that dog would still go upstairs every night right at nine o'clock. He'd go to her bedroom and sleep on the same rug just like he always did. You tell me, was Rex still taking Grandma to bed, or what? I'll tell you another story that Ernest swears is true. Ernest was coming home through the woods with his two dogs from night hunting when he heard a terrible racket just ahead. Said it sounded like an unearthly moaning. The sound was moving in his direction. Then he saw a ghostly form. The moon illuminated a skeletal form with a hideous face slowly coming toward him. Said it scared the hell out of him—his dogs didn't bark, just scattered and ran away. Said he ran as fast as he could, but he could hear the thing getting closer behind him. Then he came to the fast moving river, which is about 25 feet wide. He said luckily he saw a foot log and ran across it to the other side. Only then did he look back and the ghost was gone. The strange thing was that a couple of days later he cautiously walked back to the same area during daylight. Ernest said he looked up and down that river but there won't no foot log!"

A suspicious visitor to the group asked, "Then how did he get across?"

"Don't know. To this day if you ask Ernest about it, he just shakes his head and says he still doesn't know."

Burl nodded to Clay and the group was asking him to tell another story. Snake was coming out and caught Clay's eye. He looked around and motioned Clay to follow. He told Clay, "Heard something the other night, but I want you to swear to God you won't never tell where you heard it, 'cause if you do my life wouldn't be worth a plug nickel."

Clay could see Snake was frightened and said, "I promise."

"I was over at the bar the other night and Ole Rip's boys and Junior were half drunk and carryin' on with each other. I was watching TV and they won't payin' me no mind. They treat me like dirt anyway—like I'm a nobody. Anyway, Junior was braggin' 'bout his car being the fastest. He was all puffed up and said somethin' 'bout runnin' that 'nigger' off the road—them's his words, not mine. I know'd he was talkin' 'bout Mack. Now, you promise you didn't hear that from me."

"I promise and I appreciate you telling me. I don't know if the law will ever catch them, but I sure hope they do before someone else gets killed. Thanks."

Snake nodded, pulled his cap down, lowered his head and walked out with a six-pack of Blue Ribbon.

Clay couldn't wait to tell Robert. When he told him, Robert replied, "It sure ties in with what I saw."

"What do you mean?"

"I was filling up my truck at that discount station in Lynhurst yesterday and I saw Junior's red Mustang out front. Looks like the son of a bitch has put on two new chrome side mirrors—he's replaced the black ones."

"Son of a gun—what're you gonna do?"

"Guess I'll go by the sheriff's office, but I'm not sure it'll do any good."

"I guess you're right, but it's still frustrating."

Later, relaxing in his recliner with random thoughts of Troop, Mack and Sedalia, he somehow fixated on the new church that seemed to be a frequent subject of conversation. Thinking back, it was only a year ago that Burl had brought it up at morning coffee. An out of town country preacher, his wife and what seemed like an odd helper had moved into the area and taken over the renovation of a defunct rural church. They called it the Church of the Holy Redemption. The preacher, Cyrus, was a tall, gaunt, screaming, hellfire and damnation minister. He had a short, thin black mustache that looked like a caterpillar had crawled under his nose. Members said he had a charismatic personality that could mesmerize a congregation. His nickname was "Fiddler" because he would often dance across the stage playing the fiddle to an upbeat gospel song. They said Cyrus could work a congregation into a frenzy with his screaming, dancing with his fiddle and speaking in tongues. He could get the congregation shouting, swaying and clapping hands. When someone got the spirit, he would grab their neck with one hand and hit them on the forehead with the palm of his other hand, yelling "save her Jesus, be gone wicked devil" as they collapsed on the floor. His members were mostly blue collar, uneducated, poor blacks and whites. Word of mouth testimonials of his fiery, frantic sermons pulled in the gullible and the curious. He also scheduled hot, sweaty tent revivals in the summer months.

His wife was just the opposite. She was quiet and very reserved. She smiled when she had to, but it didn't come naturally. She wore no makeup, but looked like she might have at one time. Her name was Isis, but some of the congregation referred to her as "Icey." She managed to fill the role of a preacher's wife, but not very convincingly.

Bart, the third member was a mystery. He was their somewhat slow handyman who took orders from both Cyrus and Icey. A muscular man, he walked with a plodding, stooped gait. He reminded Clay of Quasimodo without the hump. He appreciated being spoken to and responded with a sheepish smile, like Dew. He had done most of the heavy lifting in renovating the church, which also had significant help from church members.

Cyrus had a knack for raising money. In converting the basement to a community room, he had raised $50,000 from businesses and individuals in Somerset County and the Evergreen community. His glad-handing and good ole boy personality was hard to turn down. Some later said it didn't look like they spent $50,000 on the renovation when most of the labor was free.

All in all, the church seemed a big success and there was talk of enlarging the chapel. There was something, though, that didn't sit right with Clay. Burl and Professor Willis said much the same thing. Oh, well, why think about a country church with all the other problems on his mind.

CHAPTER 26

Saying:
*This country ain't been right
since lawyers outnumbered cowboys.*

Robert paid a visit to the Somerset County sheriff's office and asked to speak to a detective or investigator. Luckily it was Detective Sandidge who was also looking into Troop's beating. He had heard about Sedalia's wreck in Nelson County. When he said he was there regarding Mack's wreck, Detective Sandidge looked frustrated. He ran his fingers through his receding hair, shook his head and said, "Just don't tell me it's about Ole Rip's boys."

" 'Fraid so, at least they were probably involved, but I'm here to tell you what I've seen and heard about Junior."

Robert then filled him in on finding the fresh streak of black paint on the metal strip on the side of Mack's truck body. He told him it was the same color of Junior's previous mirrors, and he told him about glass pieces and Junior's new chrome replacements. He also told him about the conversation overheard in the *He Ain't Here* bar from a confidential source. He reiterated what was well-known about Ole Rip's boys and Junior drag racing on that section of road.

Detective Sandidge expressed his frustration. "I can confront and question them, but they'll know I've got nothing—no witnesses and no hard evidence on which I can get the Commonwealth Attorney to issue a warrant. I'm sure Junior's old mirrors are long gone. Nothing would make me happier than putting those three away."

Robert followed, "I understand. I did some investigative work in the Army. Don't mention what was overheard. They might recall who could have overheard it. By the way, I heard you were handling Troop's beating."

"Afraid so, and like Mack's, unless Troop remembers something, there's no evidence."

"I know, but for what it's worth, I was able to back track to the area where it appears he was beaten."

Detective Sandidge perked up. "Really?"

"Yep. I was able to follow a trail where the leaves and brush were disturbed. There were signs of a scuffle in an area that borders Ole Rip's place. I'm sure you've heard rumors about Rip's moonshine operation. Anyway, there's a well-worn path around his property where someone constantly patrols. The scuffle area is very close to the path. Troop does a lot of coon hunting at night and might have wandered onto Ole Rip's posted land."

Robert continued, "I saw what looked like specks of blood around a log. Some areas were sheltered in the overhang of the log. Wonder if you could get some samples if you sprayed luminal around? We had some rains since it happened but it might work. I've heard luminal can show up some pretty old bloodstains."

"Don't know; what we'd probably find would be Troop's and the dog's blood."

"Maybe so, but Easel had a fresh bandage on his hand when he was seen at Rucker's store, which was right after Troop was beaten. You never know, you might get lucky."

"That is interesting. Let me think on it. Will you take me up there and show me?"

"Just let me know. It's a hell of a hike; you'll need to pack a lunch."

In a joking way, Detective Sandidge said, "Lord man, get out of here. If I didn't already have enough to worry about, you just doubled it."

"Sorry, you have my sympathy. You know how to reach me. I'll keep you posted if I hear or find anything else."

"Thanks for making my day."

Later, after Clay had called, Robert felt depressed and disappointed. He took two Aleve and collapsed on his sofa. His wife Corine noticed his somber mood and said, "Here you go again. Don't you go and do something stupid like what you did to T. Wayne." Robert slowly turned his head. "I don't know what you mean about T. Wayne, but it's not right. One of my best friends is dead and another is struggling to get back on his feet and those three jackasses are still drinking and raising hell."

"I know."

But, little did Corine know the real thoughts that were running through Robert's head.

Robert's ideas were flashing all over the place. He was a regular church member and did more than his share of helping people in need. He would take the elderly to the doctor, split wood, help fix a roof, and get their groceries if they were sick. Unlike some of those highfalutin do-gooders who just went to board and committee meetings, he didn't mind working and getting his hands dirty. Robert sometimes had a problem, though, with returning good for evil. He felt that do unto others could at times mean do unto them what they had done unto others. Wasn't there something in the Bible about an eye for an eye? For the time being, he would let his subconscious mind work on a solution. If he did any of the things he had thought of so far, he was sure he would go to jail or hell.

Clay was looking through Cecil's canned goods section when he was approached by Bull.

"Saw somethin' strange the other day. Didn't make much sense to me—maybe it will to you. Anyway, I was walkin' up the old roadbed from my house—you know the one the CCC men changed when Roosevelt put people back to work. It eventually comes back in to where the present road ends. There's a clearing there where you can turn trucks around."

Bull had Clay's full attention. "I watched from a safe distance. What I saw were two trucks backed up end to end. Both had van-type bodies with roll-up back doors and one was Rip's old truck and the other was Earl Dooley's. All I could tell at first was they were offloading something from Earl's truck into Rip's truck. When they finished, Ole Rip handed something to Earl—looked like paper money. Earl then pulled up a short distance, got out and pulled down the roll-up door and left. It was then that I could see in the back of Rip's truck. It looked like there were pallets of 100 lb. bags of something like cattle feed, sugar or fertilizer. What doesn't make sense is what it was. If it was cattle feed or fertilizer, Rip could have gone to Farm Supply and got it himself."

"I agree it doesn't make a lot of sense."

"You reckon it might be stuff to make moonshine?"

"It could be."

"Oh well, it ain't none of my business."

Clay answered, "None of mine either, but it is a puzzle. Thanks for telling me."

Bull then drifted away and Clay watched him pick up cans of navy beans, sardines, potted meat and fried apples.

CHAPTER 27

We're getting more government than we paid for.
—Will Rogers

Troop could hardly wait to move back to his cabin. For weeks he had been looking forward to sleeping in his own bed and being back with all his animals. Even though the dogs usually slept outside, this night Blue insisted on sleeping beside his bed. He awoke in the morning with Blue licking his foot, which was sticking out from under the quilt. He slowly stretched all the joints and muscles that were sore and stiff. Then he rolled to the side of the bed and pushed himself up to a sitting position. Rubbing Blue's head with one hand, he used the other to help stand up. He hobbled to the kitchen sink and looked out the window at all the trees. The morning sun was showing purple and orange over the distant hills. In spite of the aches and pains, he felt euphoric. He was finally surrounded again by Mother Nature and God's biggest cathedral. Hearing the stirrings inside, Buckshot and Ruby began whining and scratching at the door, so he let them in. It was going to be his best day in a long time.

The days flew by. Spring was emerging and Sedalia no longer needed her cane. Troop was slowly regaining his strength and was able to tend to his farm chores. He hitched up Mabeline and plowed his garden.

The next time Clay went by Rucker's he could hear Burl ranting. Like an excited country preacher, he was going on about the political mess. Burl was neither a Democrat nor a Republican. He said he didn't trust either party. Clay jokingly asked if he was a member of the Tea Party, which he hotly denied. He claimed he was a conservative and went into a diatribe about politics and politicians. He was going down his laundry list of complaints about things like paying subsidies to big oil companies, corporations setting up offshore headquarters to avoid taxes, giving foreign aid to countries that hate us, not closing loopholes that favored the rich, not passing a balanced budget, not giving the president line item veto, not paying internet sales taxes, not doing enough to cut spending and both parties focusing on party goals instead of what was best for the country. He railed about how the party in power got to make political appointments of people like judges who had supported them and weren't necessarily the best qualified. And, also, that the party in power could change congressional districts to favor their candidates and on and on.

Since there wasn't a need to disagree, there wasn't much dissension. There was one unrelated tidbit that someone mentioned. Preacher Cyrus of the Church of the Holy Redemption had been arrested and given a DUI ticket. The newspaper reported Cyrus claimed it was caused by his Oxycontin medicine for back pain, but the state trooper said there was a strong odor of alcohol.

CHAPTER 28

Neither Orville nor Wilbur Wright had a pilot's license.

When Sedalia's phone rang, the muffled voice said, "Next time you won't be so lucky, bitch!" and hung up. She was stunned. The caller ID displayed "unknown." She knew it had to be Axle. It meant the Nelson County detective had talked to him. She felt both anger and fear and could feel her pulse racing. She called Clay and blurted out, "I just got threatened by Axle."

It took only a moment to register. Clay responded, "This is crazy. All our problems are coming from Ole Rip's bunch and Junior, and the law can't seem to do a damn thing! If the law can't do something, maybe we can."

"What can we possibly do?"

"I don't know. Maybe you, Robert, Troop and I can come up with something. I'll give Robert a call and I'm sure he'll contact Detective Sandidge again." Clay then told her about Bull seeing what looked like pallets of feed sacks or sugar being offloaded by Earl onto Ole Rip's truck.

"I told you they were somehow connected."

"Yep, you sure did."

"Oh, and keep your pistol handy. You might want to get a permit."

After the conversation, Clay settled back in his recliner and tried to put it all together. Clay was thinking about the feed sacks or sugar and recalling Troop saying the last thing he remembered was the strange odor in the woods. He also said he thought he remembered seeing in the dark what looked like steam rising above the tree line. Could it have been from the still? If so, the cave would have to run further behind the barn than anyone had imagined. Large volume moonshiners these days used propane so there was no smoke, but there could be steam and it would be vented along with the smell. Another puzzle was that now you could buy moonshine at ABC stores so it didn't make sense to keep cooking in the woods, but then, the store price was a lot higher.

The thoughts caused Clay to reminisce about growing up and hearing stories about moonshiners, revenue agents and moonshine runners. In those days most of the makers did it to make a living. There was pride in making good "shine" and in their minds the only thing they were violating was taxes. One old time sheriff in the neighboring county said he left them alone and they did the same. He said he knew them and they made good stuff. Clay remembered hearing about Franklin County south of Roanoke. He once heard a radio announcer jokingly say there were more bears in Franklin County than people and there were more revenue agents than bears.

In those days revenue agents were frequently checking merchants and suppliers for high sales of sugar, yeast, malt and Atlas, Mason and Ball canning jars. In most cases the producers knew the agents and vice versa. There was seldom any gunplay except in the famous Franklin County conspiracy. Brandishing a gun could add ten years to a sentence. If caught, most moonshiners accepted their fate, went peacefully to court and resumed their craft when they got out. There were instances when the revenue agent would give the moonshiner a ride to court on the day of the trial. One of the ways the women notified the men making moonshine was to go out and start calling the cows if there were revenue agents in the area.

Wondering about the current business of making moonshine, Clay Googled "moonshine" and found a multitude of web sites that included recipes, history and where you could get instructions to build your own still. There were sites where you could buy completely assembled stills. Some of the history was also interesting. Problems for moonshine began because the government lost tax revenue. Also, some unscrupulous producers began to add hazardous ingredients. To increase the kick, additives included lye, embalming fluid and formaldehyde. To increase the proof, they would sometimes add one or two pints of rubbing alcohol or paint thinner, which has methyl alcohol, or wood alcohol, in it. The drinker's body converted the methyl alcohol to formic acid, which in some cases caused blindness. One of the worst pollutants was lead. Yeast in the mash converts a portion of the alcohol into acetic acid. When the acid hits the lead in the solder used to join seams in the still, some of it forms lead acetate. Lead accumulates in the body because it can't expel it. Too much lead works on the nervous system and muscles, which causes problems ranging from colic to blindness, paralysis, convulsions and death. Some producers even used auto radiators as condensers, which contain lead. It has been said that an eagle eating just one lead shot from a kill can die. It is also said someone drinking can't tell the difference in the brand of alcohol after a couple of drinks so a bartender might serve a name brand like Jack Daniels first, then switch to moonshine that had been colored with Coke or Pepsi. Clay decided a long time ago he would never take a drink of moonshine unless he knew the maker.

CHAPTER 29

Church Bulletin:
Don't let worry kill you off—let the church help.

The death of Mack and the hell-raising by Ole Rip's boys and Junior were eating at Robert. He couldn't imagine how the law would ever stop them. The paint streak on the truck, the new mirrors and what Snake told Clay was all the evidence he needed. Again, how could he do something that might teach this bunch a lesson? He needed a plan—maybe he could do something when they were drag racing. If he took his deer rifle and found a place with a good view overlooking where they usually raced, would a bullet through the radiator into the engine cause it to blow? Maybe, but there might be a telltale hole in the grill or radiator. If he put a scope on his 30-30 Remington, could he hit a front tire on a fast moving target? Would he even need a scope?

Robert took his rifle and some bullets and went out in the woods far enough not to be heard. After zeroing in the rifle, he found he could consistently, on a rest, hit a tin can at fifty yards. It would cut down the angle of his oncoming target if he was close to the road because it would be more of a straight ahead shot. He wondered how much he would have to lead to hit a fast moving target. If he missed, he probably wouldn't have time for a second shot. There was no worry about the noise because the roar of the engines would cover the sound. Would the bullet go through the tire and show on the rim? Even if it did, would anyone notice?

Robert drove the race stretch many times to see the places that offered the best view and cover. There were several wooded hills that offered good cover. He would need to park his truck somewhere close by and walk in and out unseen. He knew they liked late Saturday afternoons, but there wasn't any set time or pattern—he might have to wait a good while. And some Saturdays they didn't race, or raced after dark. Robert knew he had to have a good excuse to tell Corine and Ant Mabel. Maybe he would start talking about going fishing or spring gobbler hunting. He hoped they wouldn't question why he changed from hunting turkeys with a rifle instead of his double-barrel shotgun.

CHAPTER 30

He has Van Gogh's ear for music.
—Billy Wilder

Thinking about Sedalia being less than her usual upbeat self, Clay tried to think of something to lift her spirits. Maybe she would enjoy a chamber music concert at the Garth Newell Music Center in Bath County. Clay asked and she gladly accepted. Clay told her about the Archduke Weekend they have each spring. It is a prelude to their main season, which runs from July through early September, every Saturday evening and Sunday afternoon. A gourmet dinner was optional after the concerts. All the music on the Archduke Weekend would be Beethoven and Sunday's concert included his Archduke piece (B-flat major, Op.97).

Clay was ecstatic. He loved being a tour guide to the western part of the state. He enjoyed the Lexington area as much as he did Charlottesville, Roanoke and Lynchburg. The ride would also give them a chance to ponder all the details about Troop's, Mack's and Sedalia's ordeals.

He picked her up early Sunday morning so they would have plenty of time for the two-hour drive. With a Beethoven CD playing in the background, Clay pointed out some of the places of interest in Lexington. First, he talked about Robert E. Lee's tenure at Washington and Lee and his tomb in the Lee Chapel and where his horse, Traveler, was buried outside. Clay joked about them finding an occasional penny placed on Traveler's grave with Lincoln's likeness facing down toward his rear end. He told her about the lemons on Stonewall Jackson's grave that are placed there by someone at night. Jackson believed foods that taste bad were good for you. One historian said Jackson couldn't have gotten lemons in Lexington, but another historian said when Custer was quartermaster for the Union Army, he got lemons through the port of Baltimore. So maybe he could have—lemons have a long shelf life. She knew about the George C. Marshall Museum and they stopped by the Virginia Horse Center to pick up an events schedule for the coming season. The conversation was interesting and engaging. Sedalia, in one of her analytical moods, was trying to put it all together. She rehashed the events that happened like Easel hanging around Rucker's, the trail in the woods, paint scrapes, Snake's comment, sacks being unloaded, glass shards, etc. Clay added, "And don't forget Easel's hand was bandaged the first time he came to Rucker's."

By now they were passing through the small picturesque community of Rockbridge Baths. Clay said a former NASCAR driver, Rick Mast, lived there. He also commented, "And don't forget the two new mirrors on Junior's Mustang and Mack's wreck looking like he was run off the road."

Going through Goshen Pass, Sedalia was fascinated by the rocks and boulders that the Maury River had carved over the centuries. She continued, "Ole Rip has to have a big moonshine operation. How else could Axle and Rance afford to spend so much on new trucks and souped-up cars? And the sugar or cornmeal unloaded tie Earl in somehow and explains where some of his money comes from."

By now they were going by Millboro Springs. Clay told Sedalia about Ft. Lewis Lodge nearby and its secluded setting on over 3000 acres on the pristine Cowpasture River. Fly fishing, hiking, canoeing, tubing, biking and delicious food adds to the ambiance. There were remnants of a small settlement nearby called Williamsville that is now almost a ghost town.

They rode and talked and Clay added, "Remember Troop said something about his last memory of seeing what he thought was steam rising, and smelling something sweet like fermenting cornmeal?"

Soon they were going over the mountain and down to Warm Springs. Turning left on Rt. 220, one of the first places they passed was the bath houses—one for men and one for women. Swimsuits are optional. He pointed out the deteriorating conditions of the historic buildings. The Homestead resort owns the baths, but locals say they aren't sure when repairs will be made. The economy has hurt the area, but new construction of something like a water park for kids was planned for The Homestead.

Soon they turned and went up the winding road to Garth Newell. The setting high on the side of a mountain alone is enough to inspire tranquility and solitude. Clay bought glasses of wine which they sipped as they socialized and waited for the concert to begin.

Sedalia was enthralled with the music and enjoyed the performance and the atmosphere. In spite of the upscale luncheon that looked enticing, they decided to eat in Lexington on the way home. To come back down to earth, Sedalia selected a Willie Nelson CD that included "On the Road Again," "The Party's Over," "Crazy," "Good Hearted Woman," and others he had written or co-written. They tried to focus on what, if anything, they could do to get justice, but it all seemed hopeless. Law enforcement seemed stymied. Everything they thought of seemed traceable back to them. It seemed depressingly futile.

After a late lunch at The Palms in Lexington, they drove home. Sedalia, in a daydreaming mood, mused, "The music was so peaceful, yet invigorating. It made me remember my younger days. I used to fantasize about living in Paris in the early 1900s. I saw myself as a writer, or artist, living the avant-garde life and being in the company of Gertrude Stein and Alice Tokias and all their friends. I imagined late night heady discussions and smoke-filled café parties with people like Cézanne, Picasso, Hemingway,

Matisse, Renoir, Fitzgerald—the names just rolled out—Cole Porter, Monet, Salvatore Dali. So many interesting people for such a short time."

Clay listened to every name and realized there was a depth to Sedalia he had not known before. Groping for a response, he replied, "It must have been an exhilarating and stimulating time and place," and then asked, "What did you study in college?"

She grinned and said, "No, it wasn't art history. I wanted to be an archaeologist, but I settled for English so I could get a job teaching."

When Clay dropped off Sedalia at her house, she took Clay's hand and squeezed it tightly. She leaned over and gave him a quick kiss on the cheek and exclaimed, "This has been the most enjoyable day I've had in a long, long time. Thank you so much—I had no idea there were so many beautiful back roads in Virginia."

Clay knew he was blushing. He drove home still feeling a warm glow.

CHAPTER 31

Saying:
Coincidence is when God chooses to remain anonymous.

Robert had been going over and over the details of his plan—how to walk in unobserved off an old logging road, how to go to and return from his stand without leaving a trail, being prepared to wait as long as necessary, not leaving any signs like wrappers, empty bottles or shell casings. Saturday afternoon seemed like the best time. The first Saturday, after selecting a secluded spot with a good line of vision, he waited four hours till the sun was going down. The waiting gave him ample time to agonize over what he was planning to do. Several times he believed the risks were too high and wondered if he shouldn't abandon the idea. On the second Saturday, still having the same doubts and about ready to call it a day, he heard the distant rumbling of high powered engines coming his way. The boys were warming up.

Junior had his '67 red Mustang and Axle had his '69 Camero. They let Rance rev up his Ford dually so he could feel included, but he never raced. Both Junior and Axle had fine-tuned their cars and added heavy-duty shocks, struts and springs. They souped-up the existing engines and added bigger carburetors, heavy-duty cams and wide rear tires.

Robert watched them make practice runs. When it got serious, Rance would be on the hill to watch for other vehicles and police and give them the start signal.

Robert had been trying to guess how much to lead the front tire, and practiced moving the barrel as they warmed up. Even a shot just in front of the tire could ricochet up and cause a blowout.

He then heard the sound that meant the big race was getting ready. He realized his hands were sweating and shaking. He heard the tires squeal and an explosion of loud engines. He saw them coming down the hill wide open, side by side, in a dead heat, crossing the bridge where Mack was killed and coming flat out straight at him. Junior was in the near lane. Robert was close to the road, but well concealed. He slowly tightened his trigger finger and led the right front tire on Junior's Mustang. And then he fired! The sound was muffled by the roar of the engines. For a moment he thought he had missed, but then he thought he heard a tire blow. He saw a puff of smoke or dust and the Mustang swerved as Junior tried to pull it back on the road. He overcorrected and sideswiped Axle's car. Axle careened off the opposite side and with dust and gravel flying everywhere, he went over the bank. Junior was losing it. He got sideways and rolled twice before going off the road and hitting a big poplar tree. After the scraping, screeching and crash sound, there was an eerie silence as the dust and smoke settled. Axle was struggling out of his car as Rance came racing to the scene.

Robert wanted to watch but knew he had to leave. The wreck was worse than he expected. He hoped Junior wasn't dead but knew it was possible. Making sure he left no telltale signs, he pocketed the empty shell and carefully picked a different way back to his truck to avoid the look of a trail. By the time he got back to his truck fifteen minutes later, he could hear sirens in the distance. Somehow he would have to look tired, but calm and composed when he got home. He knew Corine, however, would be suspicious—she could always read him like a book.

CHAPTER 32

If they put his brain in a bird, it would fly backwards.

The next day the local TV news and newspaper described the wreck. The state trooper believed they were drag racing and charges would be forthcoming. Junior Dooley was reported in serious but stable condition. Axle had been released with cuts and bruises. Someone said he had a couple of broken ribs.

It was the main conversation around Rucker's and the community. There was some sense of relief that maybe the roads would be a little safer for a while. Sedalia had mixed emotions because she knew it wasn't over with Axle.

Holding the morning paper, Corine gave Robert a suspicious look and said, "Don't reckon you'd know anything about this either."

"About what?"

"There was a bad wreck on the Piney River road yesterday—says that Dooley boy is in intensive care."

Looking surprised, Robert answered, "Well, I be damn," and then, "it couldn't have happened to a better person."

"Humph."

A couple of days later Clay picked up Troop to ride down to Rucker's for morning coffee and groceries. Conversation among the group still centered on the wreck. Burl was saying, "Junior had it coming. They say he's going to live, but he's really busted up—broke both his legs, his right arm, several ribs and lots of stitches on his face—had to sew his nose back on."

Walter added, "Axe, Axe, Axe ain't gonna look, look, look too, too pretty ne, ne neither."

Burl said, "Axle has tried coming over in my lane a couple of times to see if I'd give way, but I always hold my ground and he backs off—hell, he knows he couldn't win against a dump truck—that'd be like takin' a pocketknife to a gunfight."

As the conversation wandered, Clay noticed Easel standing in the shadows down one of the aisles. Troop had gotten a basket and was going around getting his groceries. Clay watched as Troop came down the aisle where Easel was standing. He had to come close to Easel in order to pass. After he went by, Troop seemed to hesitate for a moment. It was more like some sensory response. He then continued shopping and took no further notice of Easel.

Afterwards, as they were riding home, Clay noticed Troop was unusually quiet. "What's wrong, Troop? You look lost in your thoughts."

"Don't know—sometimes I see or feel things I can't explain—sort of like what I told you about in the hospital. I don't know, that mean lookin' tall man. I felt somethin' when I walked by—he smelled funny, too."

"Yeah, I know. Cecil calls him 'Stinkbug'."

"Right, he did smell right rank; who is he?"

"That's Ole Rip's brother, Easel. We've seen him at Rucker's several times since you got hurt." Clay continued, "Don't know if I should tell you, but Cecil, Robert and I wonder if he knows something about what happened to you. We wonder if maybe he wasn't the one who did it. He did have a fresh bandage on his hand the first time he came by Rucker's after you got hurt."

Troop was silent for a moment, and then asked, "Why would he do somethin' like that?"

"Maybe you were getting too close to Ole Rip's moonshine operation. Remember what you said about the smell and the mist above the trees? Robert and I wonder if the vent to the still is close-by."

Troop seemed bothered by what he heard and Clay worried that maybe he shouldn't have told him.

CHAPTER 33

God's language is silence—everything else is bad translation.

Back at the cabin, Troop sat on his porch the rest of the afternoon and thought about what Clay had said. The more he thought, the more he worried. Even after sundown and darkness covered the mountains, he kept wondering why. There was only one thing to do; he needed to go back to where it happened. It would be a long, hard walk, but he was slowly getting stronger and he would take his time. He remembered the night and how far Blue had run that coon. He remembered the wind picking up and sitting on a log to rest and listen. At times Blue had gone out of hearing range only to come back in range. Troop knew the mountains like the back of his hand, and he knew how to get there. The next day the agony continued. He would do it tomorrow.

Buckshot and Ruby would stay if Troop told them, but he had to put Blue in the feed room. After putting a ham biscuit and two cookies in his pocket, and getting his new walking stick, he started. He knew places where he could get good clean water. The morning was cool, but he knew it would get warmer. As he walked he couldn't help thinking that who beat him didn't care if he lived or died. And why would Easel, or one of Rip's other employees, need to patrol late at night. Troop took his time and stopped to rest when needed. Eventually he came to the ridge where he was sure it happened. Not knowing exactly where the patrol path was, he shifted into the hunter mode. Troop could move through the woods as quietly as any forest animal. His hearing was acute and he could walk through leaves without making a sound or snapping a twig. He moved slowly over the crest of the ridge, stopping frequently to look and listen. He wondered how anyone could have sneaked up behind him and not be heard. The wind must have covered their sound.

As he looked and listened, he carefully scanned the general area. Then he spotted the log he believed he had been sitting on. From there, he slowly went over the crest of the ridge and saw the worn path. Well concealed and without moving or making a sound, he watched and listened. In the distance he saw a movement and recognized the man he had seen at Rucker's. Troop then got a good facial view and the man looked evil. He watched him follow the path until he was out of sight.

He went back and sat on the log. There was that faint, sweet odor of cooking fermented cornmeal—the vent must be nearby. He studied the surrounding area and saw something familiar lying under a distant bush. It was his old walking stick.

Troop was a peaceful man. Always polite, calm and friendly, no one had ever seen Troop show anger. Even if slighted, he didn't hold a grudge. But this was different—he would have aches, pains and bad memories till the day he died. This was something that couldn't go unanswered.

CHAPTER 34

He was always the first to sit down in spelling bees.
—Anonymous

Spring was turning to summer. Clay was thinking about cutting hay soon when the phone rang.

Rucker's store showed on the caller ID.

"Hey, Cecil, what's up?"

"Something a little weird. Thought I'd better give you a call. A man coming down Spruce Creek saw something unusual. Said there was a car in the ditch with the driver's door open and it sounded a lot like Sedalia's Jetta. It just doesn't sound right. Thought you might want to check it out."

"I agree; I'm on my way."

Clay tried her home phone and cell phone and there was no answer. He drove up Spruce Creek Road and soon saw Sedalia's car. It appeared she slid in the ditch at a 45-degree angle with the passenger side bumper embedded in the bank. His first thought was that maybe she walked home so he rushed to her house, blew the horn, then stuck his head in the door and called loudly. No answer. His concern intensified.

Going back to the Jetta, he looked more closely. Then he saw her handbag on the floor—something she'd never leave behind. The gravel around the door was recently disturbed. Something was not right. There were wide tracks in the road that looked like a vehicle had scratched off. Clay went back to Rucker's and told Cecil what he'd found. Cecil said there was one more thing that another customer had said that he forgot to mention. He said he'd seen a big black Ford dually hightailing down Spruce Creek Road.

Instantly, Clay knew something bad had happened. He told Cecil about Axle's threatening phone call. Then Cecil became alarmed and exclaimed, "Let's call the sheriff! Do you think that damn Axle is brazen enough to kidnap her in broad daylight?"

"You call and I'm going toward Ole Rip's place and if I don't see his truck, I'm going in!"

"Don't you think you'd better wait for the sheriff?"

"Can't wait. You tell'em to send someone with a four-wheel drive!"

"Watch yourself. That bunch would just as soon shoot you as look at you."

His mind racing, Clay drove fast, hitting seventy and eighty, plus. There was no sign of the dually. When he finally reached Ole Rip's road, he saw fresh signs where a vehicle recently splashed water out of the mud holes. The main farmstead was about a mile from the entrance. The road in was so rough a regular car couldn't go over the high berms unless you went over at an angle and even then you might lose your oil pan. As Clay went over a high knoll, he looked down a long steep grade and saw the tailgate of the dually sticking out of a thicket beside the road. The cab was hidden in tall weeds beside an old building.

Clay hesitated. If Axle had Sedalia inside, he knew he should walk in as quietly as possible. He was thinking, damn, why didn't I bring my gun? He parked his truck and looked behind his seat. The only thing he could find was a long handle adjustable wrench and a crowbar. He took the wrench, got out, and closed the door softly. In the distance he could hear Ole Rip's pack of dogs raising Cain. He hoped they wouldn't come this far from the house.

Moving silently along the road, he approached the rear of the dually. There was a fresh path of mashed down weeds to the old building. He thought he heard muffled sounds. He moved slowly toward the building. There were narrow gaps between some of the boards. He edged up to a crack where he hoped he could see without being seen or heard. It was dark inside except where slivers of light here and there came through holes in the roof and where a board was missing or hanging sideways.

He heard the sounds of scuffling and kicking. Then he heard a voice.

"You be good and I not hurt you." Clay froze. It wasn't Axle's voice. It had to be Rance!

What the hell! He rammed open the flimsy door with the wrench raised to strike. The scene was crazy. Sedalia was tied up and gagged with duct tape. Rance was pulling on her clothes as she tried to kick him off. In a flash, Rance rose and blocked his swing and hit Clay with his right fist that sent him sprawling. He tasted blood in his mouth and felt it running down the side of his face. Dazed, he tried to rise, but Rance knocked him down again. He seemed like a wild animal. Sedalia, down to her panties and bra, was turning and twisting and trying to crawl or somehow divert Rance's attention.

It dawned on Clay he didn't have a chance. Rance was strong as an ox and he was used to lifting heavy limbs and loading logs. He realized his only hope was to fake unconsciousness, so he curled in the fetal position and put his arms around his head.

Enraged and wild-eyed, Rance kicked him in the back and stomach and was getting ready to kick his head when he saw Sedalia turning and rolling across the floor. His attention shifted and he ran over and grabbed her. He slapped her hard across the face and screamed, "Sit still!" She continued to squirm and twist and hoped it would give Clay time to recover. Rance saw the tears running down her cheeks. He suddenly became child-like. He seemed to feel a sense of compassion and he put his arms around her. She pretended to resist, but realized that he was calming down. Looking over his shoulder, she watched Clay very slowly moving his arms and taking in the situation. Rance glanced around and saw that Clay still looked immobile. Then, like a child, he began rubbing her head and talking to her like she was a puppy or a kitten. Still holding her, he started rocking back and forth and humming some song he must have remembered from childhood.

Clay, seeing his chance, slowly began to reach for the wrench. Rance now seemed to be in an imaginary world and didn't notice the soft sound of creaking boards. Clay picked up the wrench and slowly stood. He delivered a hard blow to the back of Rance's head, who fell over and went as limp as a dishrag.

Clay held Sedalia and pulled off the duct tape as she leaned her head on his shoulder. Then he untied her hands and feet and got her skirt and blouse. He helped her put them on and they stood there holding each other, with Sedalia sobbing.

Simultaneously, they heard the sirens coming along the road and the pack of dogs coming from the farmhouse.

Two deputies arrived before the dogs and had their guns ready. Ole Rip, who was just behind the dogs, was sizing up the situation and trying to call off the dogs, but one leaped toward a deputy who shot it in midair.

The deputies then rushed inside with Ole Rip right behind. Clay told the deputies that Rance had kidnapped Sedalia, had brought her here and was pulling off her clothes when he came in. Also, that Rance had beaten and kicked him. They could see the cut on his face and red spots where he had been hit on his arms and face. He wasn't sure about the pains in his ribs, stomach and back. They cuffed Rance, who was starting to show signs of consciousness, and took him out to the SUV. Ole Rip went into a rage and said they "won't taking Rance nowhere." One of the deputies, who was tall, lean and fit, got in Ole Rip's face and said, "Unless you want to be charged with interfering with an arrest, the best thing you can do is back off!" Showing the taser, he said, "You see this? All I've got to do is touch you and you'll be laying as flat as that man was."

Ole Rip was fuming, but he wasn't stupid. He backed off, grumbling as the Lynhurst Life Saving Crew came in and helped Sedalia in their van to go to the hospital. Clay asked if he could follow in his pickup. One of the attendants he recognized answered, "You ride in here with her and the other attendant and I'll drive your pickup. See you at the ER."

CHAPTER 35

Last words of James Rodgers when asked if he had
any last request before being shot by a Utah firing squad:
"Why yes—a bulletproof vest."

Time was flying and things were happening fast in Lynhurst
and Evergreen. The next morning the coffee group was abuzz with
the abduction of Sedalia by Rance and the exciting rescue by Clay
and the county deputies. They figured Ole Rip might be getting a
little worried. On top of that, one of Earl Dooley's tractor-trailers
with a load of watermelons had wrecked last night. It happened just
north of Chatham on Route 29 between Danville and Lynchburg.
Clay jokingly quipped that Chatham was close to Tight Squeeze,
Loose Grip and Climax. Because it happened late, the morning paper had only a brief statement. It said there were no injuries and
that the accident was under investigation. The group was sure Earl
was well insured. There was a lot of concern about Sedalia. She had
not fully recovered from the trauma of her wreck and now there
was the abduction. Clay said she had been given a sedative and was
now resting. The group speculated that Rance would be commit-
ted for a psychological evaluation and probably be charged with
abduction and attempted rape. In any case, he wasn't going to be
released on bail.

The morning coffee group conversation had certainly been
more interesting than usual. On the way home Clay heard a bulletin on a local radio station about the watermelon wreck. It seems
investigators had uncovered a cache of marijuana hidden with the
watermelons. This was really big local news and since it was inter-
state commerce, speculation ran the gamut from the State Police

to the FBI being called in. The announcer said they were trying to get in touch with the truck owner, Earl Dooley, of Evergreen.

The six o'clock TV news was more comprehensive. It was carried as the lead story on the Lynchburg, Roanoke and Charlottesville stations. Mr. Dooley was quoted as saying he had no idea how the marijuana could have been on his truck. He suggested that since it was a backhaul it might have been something arranged between the shipper in Nogales, Arizona, and the receiver, a large produce distributor in Baltimore. He said his contract was only to pick up and deliver the watermelons. The reporter asked Mr. Dooley if he thought his driver might have been involved, but he said he didn't think so. No charges had been made against the driver, except failure to control his vehicle, and the investigation was ongoing. An investigator questioned said that like the large ocean-going containers used in international shipping, there was no way to know all the contents being shipped on tractor-trailers.

Back at his cabin, Troop had been agonizing over his trek and what he had found. In spite of his peaceful nature, his anger toward Easel was growing and he couldn't stop thinking about what he could do. There had to be some way to break up the moonshine operation. The authorities, along with local people, had believed for years that something was going on, but no one was sure of how it was done. Maybe he could notify a revenue agent through the sheriff's office. But even if they believed him, the best he could hope for would be a shut down of the operation. Ole Rip would get fined and maybe some jail time, but it wasn't enough. Easel and Axle would probably go free and could set up another still in some hidden hollow and be back in business in no time. There had to be a better way. He could pour gasoline down the vent and light a fire, but he knew the still had to be a good ways from the vent opening.

During his life, Troop had worked for a number of local farmers, orchardists, contractors and timber companies. One of those companies where he had worked built and repaired state roads and bridges. Dynamite was used numerous times to break up big rocks and loosen large tree stumps. Troop knew how to put the cap and fuse to the dynamite and was one of the people the company trusted to plant the explosives. He knew dynamite was strictly controlled, but he thought about getting in touch with his old boss that still ran the company. Maybe, just maybe, something like that might work, but then again, maybe not.

CHAPTER 36

Church Bulletin:
Low Self Esteem Group will meet Thursday at 7:00 p.m.
Please use back door.

Days drifted by. Sedalia didn't feel Axle would be a threat for at least a month or two. Rance's case was starting to progress. The judge had sent him to Central State Hospital in Petersburg for psychological evaluation. Sedalia tried not to think about the eventual trial ordeal. She knew Ole Rip had the resources to hire a big time defense attorney. The only other news was about Cyrus, the preacher they called "Fiddler." He hadn't been seen or heard from for a couple of weeks. Church members were told he was recuperating from back surgery in West Virginia. Icey hadn't been seen lately, either.

Clay believed Sedalia was slowly making progress until he went by one morning to see if she needed anything. When she came to the door she looked like death warmed over. Her face was swollen, her hands were shaking and he could tell she'd been crying. She started to speak, then broke down. Clay put his arms around her as she let it all come out. After crying she said she hadn't had a good night's rest since it happened. "All those pills make me feel like an addict. I sleep all day and stay up all night. Some dreams are surreal. I keep seeing that monster chasing me and smelling his body odor and bad breath." Clay asked if she had talked with a counselor or psychiatrist and she blurted out, "He's the one that prescribed all those damn pills. He really acted like he didn't have time to listen. I'm not going back!"

Clay replied, "There was an old judge in Lynchburg that used to say he'd never known a psychiatrist that didn't need one." He thought a moment and then said, "Would you feel better if one of those ladies who were here after the wreck came over and spent nights for a while?"

"I might, but I don't want to be an invalid. I don't know. They are nice, but they're strangers. Everything is so confused. I don't want people to think I'm crazy."

"I don't know if this makes sense either, but I'd be glad to come over at night and stay in your extra bedroom until you feel better."

"I don't want you to do that. Besides, what would people say?"

"They'd say Clay got lucky. Seriously, they wouldn't say anything. No one needs to know. I can answer my cell phone over here as easily as I can at home. The few people who call my landline phone know they can get me on my cell phone, or leave a message. Besides, as you and most of my friends know, I'm notorious for not checking messages."

A long silence, then, "I don't know. Maybe we could try it a night or two. You sure you don't mind? It's a terrible imposition."

"No problem and you can change your mind anytime. I'll come over around eight."

"I feel like a fool, but okay."

"And don't fix anything. I'll eat before I leave home."

"OK, it's a deal."

"Now, is there anything you need at Rucker's or in Lynhurst?"

Sedalia thought and wrote down a few things on a scratch pad and gave it to Clay and then said, "Scratch the Ben Gay and add 5mg. of Melatonin."

CHAPTER 37

My wife and I had words. I didn't get to use none of mine.
—Anonymous

Seemingly unrelated things were going on in the community. Robert took Detective Sandidge on the long hike to the area where Troop was beaten. There were only faded blood specks here and there, which he sprayed with Luminol and collected. Detective Sandidge wasn't optimistic because of the time lapse and light rain and he suspected it would be Troop's and Blue's blood. Robert showed him the trail Ole Rip's guards travelled and warned him they needed to stay out of sight in case one of the guards should come along.

In the meantime, Troop decided to call his old construction foreman, Mr. Roakes. He got Cecil to dial the number. He asked Mr. Roakes if there was any chance of getting three or four sticks of dynamite to blow up a large oak stump in his garden.

Mr. Roakes answered, "Troop, you know that's illegal."

"Yessir, I know, and I wouldn't ask if I was able to bust it up myself. Guess you heard 'bout me gettin' beat up."

"Yeah, I did. Sorry to hear 'bout it. How you doin'?"

"Doin' better, but I'm still not strong. Don't know if I'll ever get my full strength back."

"Well, okay. We'll be workin' on a bridge up your way next week. How 'bout I meet you 'round lunchtime on Tuesday at Rucker's? I'll also bring a couple of caps and fuse."

"I'll be there."

"You know this conversation never happened."

"Yessir, done forgot it already."

With all the goings on, Clay remembered things he said he was going to do and hadn't. He had promised Ant Mabel he was going to bring Sedalia by for a visit and he had planned to get another horse to keep Pepper company. Maybe he could adopt a horse from one of the animal rescue places. With the bad economy, some owners couldn't afford to keep their horses. Or maybe he would buy a donkey. Donkeys were gaining in popularity as guard animals. They bonded with the livestock and would chase off coyotes, dogs and foxes. They ate the same food as the cattle, and except for a few jacks, they were gentle. A donkey might make a good companion for Pepper.

With Ant Mabel he knew he was in trouble. Oh well, Ant Mabel would give him hell no matter what. He knew other retired people who complained about putting things off. At least things seemed to be going well with Sedalia. After the awkward first night, they settled in a routine of him arriving around dark and sitting around watching TV together. Sedalia was steadily getting her confidence back and was becoming more relaxed and talkative. Mornings changed to where she insisted on fixing coffee and breakfast.

CHAPTER 38

Whatever happened to Preparation 'G' and WD39?

On a routine truck weigh station check on Route 29 near Lynchburg, a county deputy was going down his checklist on one of Earl's trucks. Although it's called a weigh station, it is also concerned about safety requirements, like lights, brakes, tires and so forth. While walking behind the trailer, the deputy noticed a clear liquid dripping from under a rear door. He smelled and touched a fingertip to his tongue. It had a strange odor so he asked the driver what he was hauling. The driver said his shipping document included four pallets of four-one gallon cases of white apple cider vinegar. The deputy initially accepted his explanation, but then started thinking it didn't smell or taste like any vinegar he had ever tasted, so he asked the driver if he could inspect his load. The driver became belligerent and said, "Hell, no!"

The deputy scratched his head and said, "Well, I have the right to inspect any suspicious cargo, or I can put a hold on this truck until I get a search warrant." The driver simmered down and agreed. Apprehensive, the deputy called his supervisor and explained the situation. His supervisor said he'd be there in fifteen minutes.

When the driver opened the door, the smell was stronger. One of the cases on top of the shrink-wrapped pallets had somehow come loose and tipped over. A couple of the jugs began leaking when they hit the floor. The cases had the name of an apple products company in the Shenandoah Valley and were labeled "Pure White Apple Cider Vinegar." There was a big red apple label on the box and the jugs.

When his supervisor arrived, the young deputy showed him the broken jugs. The older sergeant smelled and tasted the liquid and exclaimed, "That ain't no cider vinegar—tastes like moonshine to me. I need to make a phone call."

By then the driver was getting fidgety and told the officers he was already running late and would miss his delivery appointment. The sergeant responded, "You might want to give'em a call 'cause you probably won't be making this delivery. We're gonna be mighty interested in this delivery address."

When the agent from the Virginia Alcohol Control enforcement department arrived, it didn't take long to impound the trailer. He then wrote up the particulars about the driver, his company, and the contents of the trailer and seized his shipping documents. After interviewing the driver and getting the information on the owner, Earl Dooley, he released him. The driver said he'd call someone to come and pick him up.

CHAPTER 39

I have never killed a man, but I have read many obituaries
with great pleasure.
—Clarence Darrow

Troop began putting the fuse into the cap. He taped three sticks of dynamite together, inserted the cap and fuse and made sure it was securely wrapped so it wouldn't separate if it hit an obstruction while being lowered. He tied a strong, thin rope to the dynamite to lower it into the vent hole. He hoped the opening would allow him to lower it to a good depth before it exploded. He had a fuse that burned about a foot a minute, so he cut it four feet long. He put the package in his backpack and slung it over his shoulder. He put a sausage biscuit and a cookie in his pocket. After putting Blue in the feed room, he took his walking stick, a flashlight and started on the long hike.

It was getting dark when he approached the ridge that joined Ole Rip's land. He hadn't needed the flashlight yet and could still follow a rough trail with the help of a half moon, which had just risen on the horizon. The climb was steep so he took his time as darkness slowly settled in. He knew he was out of sight until he reached the crest of the ridge, but he used the flashlight sparingly. When he reached the top, he sat and listened a long while. He didn't know how often the guard made his rounds. He wanted to wait until after the guard passed. For over an hour, he sat on the log where he was beaten. Finally, he spotted a dim light in the distance coming in his direction. He waited and watched as it passed along the path and disappeared.

With heart pounding and pulse racing, he approached where he believed the vent opening was located. He followed the sweet-sour aroma that smelled like something baking. Then he heard a noise that sounded like a jet engine. He was right at the hole. The noise meant the still was running. He had heard moonshiners say cooking with propane made that kind of sound, and the propane tank had to be put in a barrel of warm water to keep it from freezing up. It sounded like the still was some distance away, maybe too far for the dynamite to do any good.

After lighting the fuse, he tried to stay calm as he slowly lowered it down the hole. He had lowered it about twenty feet when it got stuck. Damn! That wasn't far enough. He raised and jiggled it and lowered it again. There were a couple of more snags before he was running out of line. He estimated it had been lowered about eighty feet, so he dropped the rest of the line in the hole and began running toward the log. He heard a muffled explosion and a puff of smoke shot out of the vent. Then there was silence. It didn't sound like it had done much damage, especially if the cooking was a ways from the explosion. Fearing failure, Troop stood a moment and then, dejected, started walking home.

He felt the earth give a brief quiver. It felt like a light tremor, but he sensed it came from deep within. Off in the distance, he heard another explosion. He thought he saw a brief flash of light in the sky. Not knowing what it was, he hoped it was the still, though he doubted it.

As he followed the route back home, he wondered if he had done any real damage. He became aware of sirens off in the distance. It sounded like there were several vehicles. There seemed to be an orange glow. Maybe it had worked.

The next morning his curiosity was killing him so he decided to walk down to Rucker's on the pretense of buying some groceries. When he went in the store it was full of people and everyone was talking about some big fire. Speculation was rampant. Some said Ole Rip's barn had caught on fire and burned to the ground. Another said he heard an explosion. Others wondered if Ole Rip's rumored still had blown up. Another said he heard Easel was missing. It was said that some of the outbuildings had burned because the big fire trucks couldn't get in. One said he heard they were able to save the house. One man said a fireman believed the roof of the cave behind the barn had caved in, said there was nothing but rocks and ruble. It bothered Troop that Easel was missing.

CHAPTER 40

They say you shouldn't say anything about the dead
unless it's good. He's dead. Good.
—Moms Mabley

Lots of news was happening. Each day following the fire and explosion brought more news about the investigation. Officials said they believed there had been a still working and the cave-in either ruptured a propane cylinder, or broke the line from the cylinder to the burners, causing the escaping gas to explode. The charred remains of a body believed to be Easel was found. It was estimated there had been four-800-gallon black pot submarine stills. Guessing at the production, it was estimated each still averaged about 80 gallons a week, or 320 gallons total. Using just $10 a gallon would yield $3200 per week, but Ole Rip probably got more—he made good shine.

Clay noted that "Midnight Moon" was selling for around $22 a fifth at local ABC stores. There still seemed to be a good margin in making the homemade variety.

Other unusual and seemingly unrelated things were also going on around Evergreen. The Virginia Alcoholic Control Board agents were probing the moonshine case, and the sheriff's department was investigating Easel's death. The two groups were also trying to figure out if there was any connection between Earl and Ole Rip. They were joined by an ATF agent also trying to figure out who the final buyer was, along with whether or not dynamite had been used in the explosion. Clay and Robert figured there must be other parties involved because they doubted Earl and Ole Rip had the expertise to set up this size operation.

Rumors were flying as to why "Fiddler" and Icey were still missing. Another puzzle was Axle's whereabouts. He hadn't been seen for over ten days. A side story was that T. Wayne Clifton, the lawyer serving a long jail term for the earlier murder, might get a new trial. He was claiming some evidence in his trial had been withheld or tainted.

Troop was still agonizing over Easel's death. He hadn't wanted anyone killed, even Easel. He thought about telling Clay or Sedalia, but was too embarrassed. Sedalia was improving and Clay was still spending nights in the guest bedroom. One night she had a nightmare about being chased by Rance and, in a daze, wandered into Clay's room and lay on the covers beside him. When she awoke with her arm across his chest, she realized her mistake and made a hasty retreat. Clay never woke up.

The rumor mill ramped up. Attendance at morning coffee was drawing a crowd. Even some of the local women were drifting through on the pretext of picking up a few groceries. Women at morning coffee were tolerated but not encouraged. After all, they had their own communications network that would rival the CIA. Garden and book clubs, church committees, e-mail, telephone, Facebook, Twitter and others provided a hot bed of information.

Lucy Green, the number one, uncontested gossip in the community, to everyone's dismay, was stopping by frequently. Locals called her "Lucy Lips" behind her back. Her forte was embellishment. One local said she'd rather lie when the truth would suit better. Trying to get a word in edgewise with Lucy was like wrestling a greased pig. If you saw her coming you'd cross the street. On top of lying, she was also the neighborhood critic. In a group she had a knack for turning a conversation around to one of her favorite subjects and then proceeding to dominate the conversation. Being an authority on everything, she criticized every idea no matter how good it was. She could suck the oxygen out of an

Optimist Club meeting. Burl, on the other hand, was a confessed gossip, but at least he was upbeat and gave other people a chance to talk. Most of his comments were positive, but even he said Lucy just came in to yak and see if there was anything additional to add to what she already knew. One day after she left, Professor Willis spoke up and said the word "gossip" came from an old English custom of newspaper editors sending reporters to bars to listen for interesting news—or, "go sip."

Burl jokingly said Lucy was a witch and she was putting in a lot more flying time since she got a new vibrator broom. Bull didn't get it.

CHAPTER 41

Bumper Sticker:
God, please protect me from your followers.

At the next morning coffee, the bombshell was Icey's death. Several had heard the afternoon before that she was dead. Someone said the church secretary had needed to get the key from Icey to update some church records. She had gone to Icey and Fiddler's secluded house to get the key. Icey's car was there, but no one came to the door. Thinking Icey might be in the kitchen, she went to the back door and knocked. When no one answered, she started peeping in the windows. It was then that she saw Icey's legs on the floor between the hall and the kitchen. She immediately called 911 and the county police were there in twenty minutes. She had been shot in the middle of her forehead and apparently had been dead for several days. The morning paper had only a short piece about the presumed murder. The church secretary also told the police the last she heard was that Fiddler was in a hospital in West Virginia. She said she was told he had a back operation. She mentioned that things at the church had been peculiar for some time.

The following morning the bold front-page headline read "MINISTER'S WIFE MURDERED." Other state and regional newspapers and TV stations picked up on the story. Even CNN and the *Richmond Times Dispatch* mentioned the story. The accompanying article covered the colorful Church of the Holy Redemption and its charismatic preacher, Cyrus "Fiddler" Jones. It said Isis, his assumed wife, was his strongest supporter. Clay wondered where the reporter got his information. The article said Cyrus was believed to be recovering from back surgery in a West Virginia clinic. It said the sheriff was sending an investigator that day to interview Cyrus. Several church members interviewed said the last few Sunday services consisted of a few prayers by a deacon, some hymns by the congregation, and the passing of the collection plate.

The following day's news was as shocking as the previous. The investigator who interviewed Cyrus reported that under intense questioning, Cyrus said he and Isis were not married. He said her last name was Bomano, and she was his boss. He said he was hired to start and run the church and he believed she worked for some out-of-state outfit. He really didn't know who they were or where they were located. He did say he once saw what looked like a pile of cash in a partially opened desk drawer. He also said his back was fine—that he was in a rehab facility being treated for Oxycodone addiction. He said he had never seen any of Isis' notes or records and she always closed the door when she talked on her cell phone. They lived in the same house but he lived in an apartment in the basement. He asked the investigator to check on Bart, their helper around the church. Later, the officer learned that Bart was staying in a small cabin on a cattle farm about a mile away. He had been helping on the farm in exchange for free rent.

Things seemed to be starting to unravel. The first break the investigators got was tracking the route of the moonshine. The original shipping tickets pointed to a large trucking terminal in Memphis. From there the shipment would have gone to a warehouse in Nogales, Arizona. They had been unable to tie down the name of the receiver. The investigators noticed the earlier watermelon shipment had originated through a large produce terminal also in Nogales.

CHAPTER 42

A zealous locksmith died of late
And did arrive at heaven's gate
He stood without and would not knock
Because he meant to pick the lock.
—Anonymous

Sedalia, Robert, Troop and Clay decided they needed to get together and compare notes. They met in Sedalia's kitchen for lunch. Their knowledge of Ole Rip's clan, Earl Dooley's trucking business and "Fiddler's" church was probably greater than all the investigating groups. There was no agenda—just the need to figure out what they knew and guess what might be coming next.

Clay began by saying, "We found out about Earl hauling Ole Rip's moonshine and supplies, but what possible connection could they have with Icey and Fiddler?

Sedalia added, "There might be a lot more going on than we realize."

Normally reticent, Troop commented, " 'Lease the still is shut down. Ole Rip might be wonderin' what happened. Burl said one of them 'vestigators said Ole Rip just sits in a rockin' chair on the front porch and stares at the mountains—said he seems like he's in another world or probably thinkin' back when times was better. He's still got them dogs and the Mexican couple that works on the farm. If they left he wouldn't have nobody!"

Sedalia chimed in, "It's a puzzle about Axle, too. Why would he leave, and where would he go?"

Clay replied, "I've heard he took care of the money for the timber business, so I imagine he also handled the moonshine money. Wonder who he was selling to? I doubt he got paid for the last shipment, or maybe the buyer is looking for him if he paid upfront and didn't get the goods."

Robert followed, "Good point. Either he didn't get paid or he did and the buyer wants his money back. Maybe I need to share what we know with Investigator Sandidge. He must be somewhat relieved that Axle, Rance and Junior will not be a problem for a while. He's also waiting for the blood test results. 'Course it won't make much difference now with Easel dead, but it would still be good to know. Remember, Easel might have left some of his own blood."

Clay commented, "I've never seen Evergreen so worked up and I've got a feeling it's far from over. I've heard they are going to prosecute Rance if they decide he's competent."

The group wondered about what might have been going on at the church that could cause someone to kill Icey. They commented about all the media trucks with long antennas and big booms being frequent sights along with reporters and camera crews. Reporters were interviewing any local who would talk about the still explosion, Redemption Church, or Icey's murder. They had even asked about Mack's death, Troop's beating, and Junior's drag racing wreck. If there wasn't any big national or state news, local TV and radio stations began the nightly news with the latest from Evergreen.

Because of all the diverse factors in the investigation, the sheriff decided to set up a regional homicide squad. Under an agreement with area county police departments, including the City of Lynchburg, the sheriff can request help from their departments to put together a comprehensive team of investigators. The sheriff can also call on the Virginia State Police, the ATF, and the Virginia Alcoholic Control Board if needed.

About a week later the frenzy leveled off. Behind the scenes investigators were looking into Icey's possible connections with organized crime. They were also trying to trace the numbers on her cell phone. They were unable to find any evidence to show otherwise, so it was believed the still explosion and Easel's death would be ruled an accident. Conversations at morning coffee became more subdued. Members continued shaking their heads as to how all of this could have happened in their small community without anyone knowing. Axle was still missing and had become a prime murder suspect.

A week later the morning newspaper headlined SUSPECT'S TRUCK FOUND! It was in a bold mountain stream at the bottom of a deep ravine in the mountains of Southwest Virginia where West Virginia and Kentucky border Virginia. The front of the cab was smashed in and submerged up to the windshield. The truck's body was sticking up in the air out of a deep pool in a trout stream below a waterfall. It appeared to have been driven off a cliff close to a seldom-used forestry department service road. There was no body.

EPILOG I

Last words of James French,
executed in the electric chair in Oklahoma 1966:
"How about this for a headline for tomorrow's paper? French fries."

Axle became the prime murder suspect. Investigators believed he went to demand payment from Icey for the whiskey picked up by Earl, her transporter. They believed she refused and he shot her.

Investigators, trying to follow the money, believed Icey worked for a crime syndicate that had similar schemes in the surrounding states. It included drugs, prostitution, moonshine, and cigarettes shipped north to avoid high state taxes.

Some of the moonshine was eventually tracked to a Mexican cartel that was also suspected of shipping drugs into the US concealed in agricultural products.

A very subdued Fiddler was invited back temporarily by the congregation to run the Church of the Holy Redemption, along with his helper, Bart.

Behind the scene, the FBI was vigorously following the illegal drug, alcohol, and organized crime connections. So far, no arrests had been made.

The judge sent Rance back for additional psychological evaluation.

Investigator Sandidge received the blood DNA results that showed a match for Troop, Blue and another person who was believed to be Easel. This part of the investigation was temporarily put on the back burner.

The Task Force's investigation showed a lifestyle by Earl's family that seemed much higher than the trucking company's profits would support. With charges of hauling illegal whiskey and marijuana pending, it was no trouble subpoenaing all his personal and company tax, financial and accounting records. It was believed the IRS would find sufficient income tax evasion to levy fines and back taxes that might cause the company to be liquidated. Earl might also do time if it were proven he knowingly hauled drugs.

People said Betty Lou hasn't put the top down since this whole mess started. Burl, who likes colorful sayings, said he saw her at Kroger's and she had a puzzled look like a blind cat at a fish market. Betty Lou might lose her Cadillac and Junior might lose his toys, plus he won't have anyone to play with.

Ole Rip will have similar problems. The amount of fines and back taxes will be correlated to the estimated gallons of all the moonshine produced over the years and it will be enormous.

When told about everything, Dew's mother, Gladys, just shook her head and said, "Lordy, lordy, lordy, what's this world coming to?"

EPILOG II

Where are we going and what am I doing in this hand basket?
—Anonymous

Clay finally got around to taking Sedalia to visit Ant Mabel. Hearing of the visit, Robert and Corine found an excuse to be absent, which suited Ant Mabel just fine.

Hearing them arrive, Ant Mabel met them at the front door and seated them in the living room. Clay asked, "Why are you putting us in the living room? You always make me sit in the kitchen."

"Miss Sedalia is a proper guest. She belongs in the living room. Hired help like you belongs in the kitchen and, if you don't behave, that's where I'm goin' to put you."

They laughed and gave each other a big hug.

"Well, well, well, ain't you a pretty thing. I've been wonderin' if this rascal was ever goin' to bring you by."

"Ant Mabel, he does seem to procrastinate."

It didn't take long for the conversation to turn to all the recent goings on around Evergreen.

"Sho is a shame 'bout that woman gettin' shot. Wonder what kind of church she was runnin'?"

Sedalia responded, "She might have been using the church for things that aren't very religious."

"Well, she'll go to hell for that, and that crazy preacher, I wouldn't want him to lay his hands on me, which reminds me about a story I heard about a man at a bar claiming he could cure aches and pains by praying and putting his hands where it hurt. She said he approached one old crippled fellow and the old man said, "Get away from me—don't you touch me—I got full disability!"

155

They laughed. Sedalia mentioned how Ole Rip's boys and Junior had been such a menace. Ant Mabel responded, "They had it coming. I knew it was just a matter of time."

Clay asked, "Ant Mabel, how could you know that. Are you some kind of soothsayer?"

"What you mean, soothsayer?"

"That you can predict things before they happen."

Ant Mabel grinned. "Well, sometimes you need a little help from the spirits."

Sedalia perked up and asked, "Like how?"

"Well, I puts a little hex on'em."

Clay, still grinning with a smirk, "And how do you do that?"

"First, I got me a black cat's tooth, a buzzard's foot, and a bat's wing. Then I sprinkled some snake blood on'em and wrote Junior's, Easel's and Axle's names on paper and put it all in a bag. Then I buried it in that spooky swamp near Foggy Bottom Road at midnight on a full moon."

Clay now had a quizzical grin, "And where did you get all those things?"

"From road kill."

"Ant Mabel, I know you're lying. You wouldn't be caught dead, no pun intended, picking up road kill. You're just telling one of your tall tales."

"Better be careful, Clay. I know things. Things like yo pickup's been parked behind Miss Sedalia's barn every night. How could I know that?"

Red-faced and embarrassed, Clay sputtered, "Really, how could you know that?"

Ant Mabel let out a hearty belly laugh. Sedalia was also embarrassed, but she said, "Ant Mabel, I can tell you've got the "gift" and I think you know that I know. I feel it, don't you?"

"Yeah, I think so, and you got it, too."

Clay stood up. "What the hell is going on here? I'm trapped between two crazy people. Maybe you two can get Fiddler to join your coven—y'all could start your own psychic church."

"You better behave, Clay. Sedalia and I might put a spell on you."

"What are you going to do—stick pins in a doll with my name on it?"

"I was really thinking more along the line of sticking them in a monkey."

Sedalia laughed out loud.

Clay said, "I've had enough. I'm getting out of here."

"How you gonna do that—I got your keys."

"How did you get those?"

"You see? It's best not to mess with Miss Sedalia and me—besides, I don't do the doll thing anymore—last time I tried it the spirits mistook who I had in mind and the wrong William, a lawyer in Charlottesville, lost his voice."

Clay spoke again. "Ant Mabel, I know you've been putting us on, but I am curious about how you knew something bad was going to happen to Junior, Easel and Axle—and what about Rance?"

"It don't take no psychic to predict something was going to happen to them three, and Rance don't count 'cause he ain't right mentally, and we don't know about Axle yet. But they been on a collision course—it was just a matter of time."

"You might be right. Axle is a puzzle, though. He could be dead, but I've heard Ole Rip has relatives in those mountains in Southwest Virginia. There are still places in that area where North Carolina, Tennessee, Kentucky and West Virginia touch Virginia. Some mountain people don't have a very high regard for the law—especially if they think the crime was justified. They have their own witness protection program."

Ant Mabel spoke up. "Let's change the subject; how is Troop coming along?"

Sedalia finally got a chance to speak. "Troop is doing fine—he still seems distant and preoccupied at times, but he's looking better."

Turning to Ant Mabel, she said, "You might have noticed that his nice white aura has returned."

"Yes, it has, and that reminds me. Robert's aura's been a little off, but it's gettin' better. He thinks I don't know what happened to T. Wayne and Junior, but I do. I think he's gettin' over it."

Sedalia and Clay weren't sure what she meant, so they let it slide.

"Well, this has been an interesting visit. Next time I might just drop Sedalia off and pick her up later."

"Sounds like a good idea, Clay. I believe Ant Mabel and I would have a lot to talk about."

"May I have my car keys back? And what's that you're holding in your hand?"

"Oh, that's my 'gris-gris'—got it from Marie Laveau's place in New Orleans. If you ever need any herbs, roots, mojo bags, portions or whatever, I'll give you the address. I recommend their eye of newt, mandrake and mugwort." She gave another hearty laugh and said, "This here's been fun. Now you two get out of here, but come back real soon."

EPILOG III

For God so loved the world he did not appoint a committee.

One morning after most of the dust had settled, retired Virginia ABC revenue agent, Wilson Reynolds, wandered into the morning coffee gathering. Cecil, Burl and Woodrow remembered him from the old days. Others in the group had a nodding acquaintance and some remembered reading newspaper articles about chases and still raids where he had been involved. He had retired sometime ago and now lived in Moneta in Bedford County near Smith Mountain Lake. The group welcomed him and wanted to know what he was doing in these parts. He said he used to come by Rucker's in the old days for coffee, Vienna sausages, pork and beans and crackers when he was working Amherst, Nelson and Albemarle counties. He said he came by because even before he retired they believed Ole Rip was "cookin'," but they could never figure out where. He said he wanted to go up and see where the barn had backed up against the cave entrance. He said he was even more surprised a still this large had continued to operate. With legal moonshine now available, there would seem to be less demand for the homemade variety, but he said the legal price left plenty of room to make a good profit. He said he reckoned Ole Rip would remember him so he didn't expect any trouble. He said the dogs might be a problem though.

It was natural for the group to ask about the old days and it turned out there was nothing Wilson liked better than telling about catching moonshiners, chasing transporters and busting up stills. He said some of his wildest and most hair-raising experiences happened when he was working the Franklin County area. When he realized he had a captive audience, the stories began to fly. He started by talking about two older men who lived near Evergreen. He said they lived in a cabin way up on the side of the mountain—said one of their agents visited them from time to time—said they were two of the nicest fellows you'd ever want to meet and they made good whiskey. Whenever this agent went to visit, he always gave their dog a snack.

On one visit no one was at the cabin so he followed a well-worn path around the ridge and saw them cookin' up this little creek—said he was able to walk right up on'em 'cause their dog, their look-out, didn't bark. When he arrested them, one of them started cussin' and said he was goin' to kill that damn dog. The agent then told them how he and the dog had become friends. In those days you had to catch 'em at the still in order to make an arrest. If they somehow got word you were coming they'd run. And if you couldn't catch 'em, they simply got away. Some of the best 'shiners and best agents were fast runners.

Wilson told story after story. He told about an ATF agent that got the seat of his pants ripped out by the owner's German shepherd. The agent also needed stitches in his butt. A few years later the "shiner" told a reporter the agents overlooked a week's work stacked in cases on his back porch. Wilson talked about drivers and chases by agents, county and state police. He said some of those drivers could straighten out the "Crooked Road."**

**The Crooked Road stretches 253 miles in western Virginia from Breaks to Rocky Mount in Franklin County. From Breaks it goes to Clintwood where the Ralph Stanley Museum is located. From there it connects with Rt. 23 to Wise and Norton and merges with Rt. 58. Next is Hiltons, home of the Carter Family Memorial Music Center. From there the Crooked Road goes to Bristol, designated by Congress as the "Birthplace of county music" Continue on to Abingdon, home of Heartwood and the Barter Theater. Stay on Rt. 58 to Independence and Galax, home of the Rex Theater and site of the Galax Old Fiddler's Convention—the oldest and largest in the world. Eight miles away is the Blue Ridge Music Center on the Blue Ridge Parkway. Continue to Hillsville and Stuart and then to Floyd. The Floyd Country Store has the Friday Night Jamboree and is

He said one driver could drive backwards as fast as some could drive forward. That driver would go flying backward and flip his car around and outrun most any car the law had. One state trooper said he could tell if a runner was hauling because the extra weight made the tires "sing." He told them about the "Franklin County Salute." He said when a driver met a cop, he'd cover the lower half of his face with his non-driving hand. That way the cop couldn't say for sure he recognized him.

Wilson told a recent story about a moonshiner who went to his still one morning and found a bear had turned over his barrels of fermenting apples for making brandy—said the bear just looked at him and wobbled away. He began leaving apples on the ground for the bear so he wouldn't turn over the barrels and it seemed to work. Thereafter, he would see the bear from time to time. Several times he saw the bear in his rearview mirror following his truck to the still. Then the revenuers blew up the still. Afterwards, he didn't see the bear when he went back. He kinda liked the bear and worried the explosion had scared him away. On the day of his court appearance, while he was waiting for his case to be called, his son came up and whispered, "Dad, the bear's back—he's okay."

With the audience on the edge of their seats, Clay thought he saw an odd movement from a man seated in the circle on his right beside Robert. Presently, Robert gave him a nudge with his elbow and pressed a finger to his lips. He then slid a large paper bag containing a jug beside Clay's chair. Putting his trigger finger through the glass ring handle, Clay slowly lifted the jug and nestled it in the crook of his arm. Turning away to his right he raised his elbow high enough to take a swig. He caught his breath as the burn

---

one of the best places in the country to hear blue grass music. The next stop is Ferrum which has the Blue Ridge Institute and Museum and Ferrum College. The final stop is Rocky Mount, the county seat of Franklin County. It is often referred to as The Wettest County in the World because of its past history of making moonshine.

flowed down his throat. With tears in his eyes, he repeated Robert's nudge and slid the jug to Woodrow on his left. Those who had taken a sip watched the bag make its way around the circle and then back to those standing. Wilson must have wondered why all of his audience was grinning. That is, everyone except the elderly local Irishman, Clancy Finnegan. His watery, blue eyes looked sad and misty. Clay thought maybe it brought back memories of young days in Ireland sitting around a turf fire at a pub sipping "holy water."

Wilson told about clever ways moonshiners outfoxed the revenuers by delivery methods and hiding the still. He told about how one hauler delivered whiskey by stacking bales of hay on each side of a flatbed truck and covering the whiskey in the middle so it looked like a farmer hauling a load of hay—said they did the same thing with pulpwood on each side and on top with whiskey underneath. Revenuers looking for stills would look along back roads for places where gravel and weeds had been disturbed—where supplies were offloaded and taken to a still. The still operators knew this and would carry the supplies on a ramp laid across the road edge to avoid leaving signs. Moonshiners also looked for any odd footprints around their stills and would stretch black thread around the bushes and scattered lime that would show revenuers' footprints. If they found footprints, the still would be moved overnight.

Wilson, in response to a question about chases, told how drivers souped-up their mostly Ford coupes with three two-barrel carburetors, an Offenhauser intake manifold and might have a Columbia rear end and heavy-duty springs. He told about how they did things like driving with lights off—how they sometimes disconnected the brake lights—how they would duck onto a side road and then come flying out and go in the opposite direction after the chaser went by.

He told about the famous cemetery still off Henry Road in Franklin County. The operator dug out a space and put a roof over eighteen eight-hundred gallon submarine stills. He covered the roof with dirt and planted grass. He then set out white-painted cinder blocks that looked like tombstones along with fake flowers. The high capacity still could produce up to 2000 gallons of whiskey a week. It couldn't be seen in the pine thicket from the road and it looked like a country cemetery from the air. When they blew the still, trees all around were covered with gallons of mash that looked a lot like oatmeal. Debris from the explosion also covered the landscape with still paraphernalia.

About this time Robert nudged Clay again and another paper poke was being passed around. Someone asked Wilson what he thought about the recent movie *Lawless*. It was adapted from a book *The Wettest County in the World* by Matt Bondurant.

Wilson said it was Hollywood and reckoned it was okay. He said the Bondurants never shot anyone and one of their elderly relatives said she heard more cuss words in that movie than she had ever heard in her entire life up to that time. A big part of the story was about the Great Moonshine Conspiracy. It involved the commonwealth attorney and the sheriff trying to force moonshiners to pay a monthly protection fee to allow transporters safe passage out of the county.

Wilson, still oblivious to the goings on around him, told a story about two moonshiners hauling gallon jugs of moonshine hidden in a tub in their car trunk covered with hog chitterlings (guts). And he told about a county sheriff who called and told the agents where to meet a man who wanted to talk to them. It turned out the young man turned his elderly parents in for making moonshine. The agents arrested them and took them to jail. They made bail and went home. Then the agents got another call later the same night from the sheriff telling them to go back and see the couple. The old woman told them they missed something—they needed to look in their son's truck and house trailer. She said her son was dealing in guns and drugs and had a still apparatus on the back of his truck. When the agents went to his trailer the son and everything but the still were gone. The old woman told them where he might be. After getting a warrant they went and found he had gone out of their jurisdiction into West Virginia. Wilson said there were two stories as to how they caught him. One was they caught him when he came back to get some clothes from his trailer. The probable story, though, was they performed a "mountain extradition" which involved getting someone to capture him in West Virginia or otherwise "strongly" encouraged him to come back to the Virginia state line where they arrested him.

By now the second jug had made its round and Clay thought he saw a few eyelids drooping. Bull looked like he was slipping out of focus. Cecil began to notice that something different was going on. He had been busy waiting on customers, but he quickly sized up what was happening.

With a red face and hands on his hips, he yelled, "All right, you bastards! Y'all trying to cause me to lose my license?" He hesitated, and then yelled, "Get your sorry asses out of my store!" Then he grinned and said, "Meet me out back at the picnic tables—this batch of chicken is ready!"

There was a shortage of designated drivers, but it was a fine picnic.

Several months later a stranger walked into Rucker's during morning coffee. Clay thought he looked vaguely familiar. The man went up to Cecil, who was talking with the group, and said, "Last year while walking the Appalachian Trail I came in here with a friend to get supplies. I was headed back to D.C. today on Route 29 so I thought I'd take a side trip to check on something I can't get out of my mind. While hiking we came upon a man in a ditch, who was almost dead, and I just had to find out if he made it."

164

Everyone stopped talking. Cecil answered, "He made it just fine," and, looking toward Troop, said, "he's sitting right over there."

Clay spoke up, "Troop, this is one of the men who saved your life!"

Troop, looking a little bewildered, got up slowly, walked over and took the man's hand. "I want to thank you for what you done. I thought I felt something when I heard you speak."

The man, looking puzzled, asked, "How could you feel something? You were unconscious."

"Don't know, just did—your voice sounded familiar."

POSTSCRIPT

Persons attempting to find a motive in this narrative will be prosecuted; persons attempting to find a moral in it will be banished; persons attempting to find a plot in it will be shot.
—*Adventures of Huckleberry Finn*
Mark Twain

GINSENG

The Chinese have been using ginseng for nearly two thousand years. Its medicinal and magical properties are legend. An old Chinese medical text states that it is a "tonic for the five viscera, quieting animal spirits, establishing the soul, allaying fear, expelling evil effluvia, brightening the eye, opening the heart, benefiting the understanding, and if taken for sometime, it will invigorate the body and prolong life."

Modern Chinese, Koreans and other Asian people use it as a tonic and to cure disorders of the nerves, lungs, and stomach. The list is endless—treating diabetes, insomnia, anemia, arthritis, malaria, headaches, sexual impotence, coughs and colds, high and low blood pressure, prevent wrinkles, etc.

The most valuable roots are old and big and resemble a man with a body, arms, legs and head. There are laws as to when it can

be dug, and a permit is required if it is dug on federal property. In Virginia it is illegal to harvest ginseng on any state or other publicly owned land. It is allowed to be harvested on private property between August 15 and December 31.

Sedalia makes a tea. Robert puts the dried roots in a bottle of Vodka and has a jigger every night. Troop keeps dried roots and will frequently break off a small piece and chew it. Clay avoids talking about whether he uses it or how he would use it if he did. Sedalia, jokingly, told him it was good for procrastination and lying.

ABOUT THE AUTHOR

Bill Tucker, born in 1936, grew up in a country store and on a beef cattle farm. After graduating from Virginia Tech in 1957 with a degree in Animal Husbandry, he served two years in the Army, one of which was in Iceland.

After his service in the US Army, he worked for twenty years at Fidelity National Bank, headquartered in Lynchburg, Virginia. Upon retiring from the bank, he purchased a commercial food distributorship which he operated for eighteen years before selling to a competitor in 1998.

His activities include writing, buying and selling antiques, tennis, guitar playing, traveling and volunteering to deliver Meals on Wheels. He enjoys reading short stories and mystery novels. His favorite writers are Cormac McCarthy and Annie Proulx.

Bill and his wife have two married sons and three grandchildren.